Under A Red Delta Sun

Sinmisola Ogúnyinka

Under a Red Delta Sun

by Sinmisola Ogúnyinka

First published by Clean Reads

Copyright © 2018

UNDER A RED DELTA SUN

This Edition by SINMISOLA OGÚNYINKA

Published by PWG Publishing, Lagos, Nigeria

Copyright © 2020

ISBN: 978-1-959835-03-5 (Paperback)

Cover Art Designed by Amanda L. Matthews

Author photo © 2019

*Dedicated to my girl, Rose, and our campaign
against girl-slavery through marriage*

Chapter One

Fifteen-year-old Asabi jumped down from the air-conditioned school bus a moment before her best friend, Temly Cole.

She giggled. "I got a reply."

Temly hopped beside her. "A reply?"

"From Ola Ajayi." Asabi quickened her pace toward the locker room. The first bell for the assembly went off.

Temly half-ran and jerked her back. "What? And you didn't tell me?"

Asabi chuckled and darted to keep her heavy school bag in her locker. Temly caught up with her.

"You little, miserable—"

"Miserable?"

"How can you keep such a—"

Asabi mimicked the school principal. "The school hall beckons, young lady."

Temly hurried off to stash her bag so she wouldn't be late to the assembly. "I'll have your neck!" She brushed past her friend and pushed through the hustle toward the school hall.

"I'll give it to you on a platter." Asabi tickled her, and Temly swatted the dainty hand off.

A moment before they entered the hall, they sobered a bit and Asabi whispered, "I just noticed as we got off the bus. I haven't even read it."

She giggled at the stunned look the information brought to Temly's face.

The teenagers had waited months to hear from Asabi's estranged father, Ola Ajayi. Social media did wonders, and though it seemed the man hardly did much online, he was there. Asabi had found him, which was a sweet relief. How else could she have?

Eni Filips, her mother, never talked about him. Asabi's only memory was being five years old and leaving him, being dragged along by her mother as she stumbled over her knock-knees. Nothing more. She had no memory of what the man was like, or why they'd left. Thankfully.

Otherwise, what would have fueled her blissful dreams about him?

After she found him as a friend on her mother's account, she'd sent a friend request.

"Penny for your thoughts," Temly whispered.

Asabi closed her eyes. "Bliss."

It was the codename for her father. Though Temly came from a "perfect" family with both parents together, in love, living in affluence with awesome caring brothers, she understood her friend's plight.

Temly's soft chuckle wafted to her ears. A friend indeed.

The dean of the school led an opening prayer and a hymn then the principal came up to make some announcements. Class representatives took a roll call and twenty minutes later, the students dispersed to their classes.

"See you after school!" Temly called out. "Can't wait."

The girls didn't take the same subjects. Asabi, more analytic, was in the science class, while spontaneous Temly enjoyed the social sciences.

Asabi walked slowly through the corridors of the massive school area, oblivious to her classmates who rushed past, wary of being late to class. Her heart thudded. This is what she had always wanted ever since her mother had married millionaire chemist and businessman, Femi Filips...yet was she sure? Life with her mother was certain; it had a pattern. With Ola Ajayi, it was totally unknown. The man could give her a better life, or worse. Though what could be worse than what she endured now?

"Asabi!" a high-pitched voice called to her.

She gazed in the direction of her caller, rolled her eyes, and braced for another confrontation. She'd told herself she would not get into these neo-violent skirmishes the last time she was suspended for three days.

She continued walking, but Mel caught up. "I saw your chats with Romeo. Leave my boyfriend alone!"

Asabi increased her pace, but the short, plump girl pulled at her sleeve. "I mean it. We'll end up both not having him, if it's what you want."

Asabi sneered. Walking fast made her silk tights rub uncomfortably just because she wasn't so thin. "You're a little fool, Mel. I don't even like him."

"Then stick to the sissy you're in love with and leave my man alone." Mel pushed her for effect and stomped off.

Asabi glowered after her, anger etched at the sides of her almond-shaped eyes. She knew how to fight. When she was enrolled in the prestigious Funmi Kuti Academy for Young Women (FKA) alongside Temly, fellow students had thought she was all glass and daintiness and Temly was the tough one. Most people discovered they were wrong. Asabi could fight, but right now, she had no time for Mel's pettiness.

Boys meant little—or nothing—to her. They crowded her, though. Her soft features and beautiful female curves struck many as being too feminine to be a troublemaker. Not if she could help it.

"My, Mel, aren't you lucky today? I'm reserving my energy for something more tangible," she muttered.

She almost crashed into a male adult who snapped, "Look where you're going."

She then walked into the school bathroom and locked herself in a stall. Her hands shook as she opened her phone. It wasn't allowed and girls could get suspended for using their cellphones in school, but Asabi couldn't wait till after closing hours. This was the most important thing in her life.

Her hands trembled, and she dropped the phone. She picked it up quickly. To her relief, no one else was in the bathroom. She sat on the covered seat of the toilet shank and gaped at the message. Her eyes teared up.

She wouldn't have known he was the one if her mother hadn't made a nasty comment on his page and she'd stumbled on it over a year ago. She couldn't even remember the comment, but it had struck a chord, and she had sent a friend request and started correspondence.

"I will meet you in Lagos," the message read. "Just let me know when."

Asabi murmured it. When? The main crux of the matter was she'd told her father she lived in Ibadan but would travel anywhere in the world to find him. She expected he would make the same offer, but her message didn't get a response. He didn't contact her for months after the preposterous offer. She was only fifteen. He must have thought she was someone else. Her mother, maybe. Eni could be so mean when she wanted. He must have investigated her.

She knew she had investigated him. He wasn't on any other platform besides Faceinst. She didn't use her real name on the account she used to contact him, and she'd told him so. He was the only one she contacted with the fake name, and only Temly knew about it.

"I will come to Lagos," Asabi typed and placed the phone on her forehead.

He didn't have personal pictures on his page, or she could have hugged him. Well, only one silhouette of a man with close-cut hair, looking into the sun. She assumed it was he.

A loud noise signified someone had entered the bathroom space. The knocking sound of a woman's heels on the wooden floor identified the entrant as either a prefect or a teacher. Neither was good for Asabi.

She slipped her phone into her skirt pocket and made a moaning sound.

"If you think you are smart, you have another *thing* coming." Only one person had this voice, and it was the mean dean of student affairs, Ms. Chisom.

Asabi opened the seat, stuffed her finger down her throat, and threw up her breakfast, making sure some got on her starched white blouse. She was good at such things.

By the time she walked out of the booth, Ms. Chisom was all soft and concerned.

Chapter Two

The two males appeared to have been knocked out after an apparent drunken binge. The younger, only a teenager, was stretched out on a mat on the barber shop floor, his eyes half-closed. The older, who could be his father or anywhere around the age, sat on a rusty barber chair with all the wheels out and his head thrown over the back, staring with bloodshot eyes at the ceiling, his long legs thrown carelessly on the worktable.

"I wonder what time it is," the younger one slurred.

"You had too much to drink last night. I found you in the gutter in front of my shop," the older said. Both laughed at what seemed to be a private joke. "Your father will have my hide after he gets through his fit, seeing you like this."

"If he gets through it." The boy swung to his feet as agile as a cat, rather than one who spent the night drinking. "It's late. They should all be out of the house now." He stood beside the man and gazed at his image in the mirror. "Not bad after a night of drinking."

"You are too carnal to be the son of a pastor. Are you sure you don't want a paternity thing done?"

He flashed a set of clean, white teeth. "Maybe I belong to you." He smoothed back his hair, did a backslide dance move, and sang a famous line from a pop star then wrinkled his nose. "What?"

This startled the man. "What?"

"The look on your face. What happened this time? You're thinking again. A woman?"

He snickered. "A woman? Why would you even think such?"

He shrugged. "A woman does to a man what nobody can do. She takes you out of your world and sets you beyond the orbit."

"*Oh*, cut it out."

"Then what's got you all strung up? I bet on my next hairdo it's a woman who got you looking all tight."

Before the man could respond, someone knocked on the door and called out, "Law! Are you in there?"

Law moved his feet off the table, careful not to topple his crowded kit, and stood. "Yeah."

"Open up. I need a quick cut."

The boy rolled his eyes. "Don't these people know you have a life?"

"A life of barbing, Fela boy."

He opened the stiff burglary door to his shop/home and then a steel door. Too many thieves in the city made shop owners extra careful about providing their own security. A net door, he insisted, should precede the security door, unlocked on a simple bolt. Fela had claimed the net had been destroyed too many times to be outside the steel door but Law didn't change his pattern.

The customer, dressed in a stiff shirt and tailored suit hurried in. "Good morning, Law. Just trim and shape." He took the seat Law had just vacated.

"Late for work?"

"An important promotion interview," the man said breathlessly.

Fela threw his hands in the air. "It's yours. Take the job!"

The customer frowned. "He's so rude."

Law chuckled and got to work. "He prophesies. Don't hate him."

The man mumbled. "Is he not the flamboyant preacher's son, Pastor Favor Peter? I see their family picture all over the internet."

"Alas, my identity bastardized." Fela smoothed back his hair again. "This baby needs a change." He winked at Law. "May I have my chance after your esteemed patron, the new director of sales?"

The customer gasped. "How did he know?" He laughed. "It's the position I'm going for. Heaven knows I've been senior manager for over eight years. Guys I taught on the job have moved far ahead, and they just would not give it to me." He eyed Fela. "How did you know? You do prophesy?"

Fela winked again. "Take it! It's yours." He bounced to the door. "See you when we see! For my new hair style, I have a dream."

Law shook his head and gently moved the stunned client's head toward the mirror and away from Fela's retreating figure.

"He can prophesy."

Chapter Three

Temly refused to stay on the school bus without her friend, Asabi.

She pushed the door open and hurried down the steps despite the bus driver's protests. Something was wrong with Asabi, though after the drama in school yesterday, she doubted some of the pretty girl's antics. But they'd spoken in the early hours of the morning, as they did most days, and Asabi had talked about seeing Temly on the bus. She rushed to Asabi's gate, one of several black iron gates on the exclusive Nelson Mandela Estate. She pressed the bell, and the gateman opened it for her.

She curtseyed, "*Bro* Wale, good morning," and rushed off to the house.

Through the kitchen from the back door, she walked along the corridor to Asabi's room. No one was in sight. She knocked, and when she got no answer, opened the door. Her friend sat on her bed, staring out the window. She was dressed in her uniform, black sandals, and light-colored tights.

Temly feared the worst. She sat on the bed beside Asabi and tapped her shoulder. "Hey."

Asabi regarded her with soulless eyes, her lips slanted upwards in an apparition of a smile. "Hey."

"Why weren't you outside waiting for the bus?"

"I decided to stay home."

"Where are your parents?"

Asabi folded her hands on her laps and took a deep breath.

"What's wrong? When we spoke this morning, you were fine. Where's Missis?" Temly's hand rested on Asabi's shoulder.

"Missis was already up, cleaning. I heard her somewhere in the house." Asabi continued to stare. "He came in—this morning. Just after we spoke."

Temly spun her around and summoned control in her voice. "How? I called about half an hour ago." She couldn't believe her ears. A deep anger rose within her belly, and for a moment, a thick lump hung in her throat.

Asabi winced. "These days he's a bit faster. He came in as you hung up. I was dressed. Went into the bathroom—" She wound her arms around her waist.

Temly's eyes pooled. She swallowed and fought for words. The look in Asabi's eyes hurt the most. Empty. Defeated. "I can't believe this," she whispered.

Asabi shrugged again. "Such is life."

Temly sprung to her feet and paced the small room. "Let me tell my parents. Please, Asabi, I can't take this anymore." Pain in her heart made her fight for air.

"What can your parents do?" Asabi's blank expression had not changed since Temly walked into her room. "I just want to live free of him."

Temly fought tears. "Okay, let's go to school. At least, we can think about this. If you don't want my—"

Asabi laughed for the first time, but it was forced. "Temly! All ready to push on, take action. Why am I not surprised?"

Her almond eyes twinkled the way Temly always loved. She was so pretty when she was happy, and it made Temly's heart bleed. "You don't deserve this pain, Asabi. A pretty girl like you doesn't."

"And ugly girls do?"

"You know what I mean."

"You're good at thinking, aren't you?" Asabi's words laced with sarcasm. "It's not so easy, young lady."

"This is not funny anymore—"

"Go." Asabi lifted her chin, but her lips quivered. "Come here after school, and we'll talk. I have a plan."

Hope swelled in Temly's heart. At least now Asabi wanted to do something about her situation. She took a deep breath. "Now you're talking." She laughed and tickled Asabi. "I'm glad you've found a way to escape this."

"I'm still thinking, and I have to be ready to act today. So, you go on. When you come back from school, we'll talk."

"No, tell me now."

Asabi shook her head.

"I know I may never understand what you go through when he touches you, but trust me, I will help you any way I can. What's your plan?"

From the first day she learned Asabi's stepfather sexually abused her, Temly vowed to do something. At the time, all Asabi asked was sworn secrecy. She couldn't even bear to let her mother know.

"With the message you got yesterday, I have a plan, too. Did you reply?" Asabi drew in a shuddering breath and shook her head. Temly sighed. "Wait a minute. Is your mother not home? Where was she when he—he came?"

Asabi exhaled. "She slept in the house last night. With him, too." She swallowed. "I don't know where she is now."

"And he had the guts to come to your room this morning? With her just across the corridor?"

Asabi nodded. "He's quiet about it most of the time. Except when she's not home." She choked on her words. "Go to school, Temly. You're running late—"

Temly wrapped her arms around her. "I'll have to get a taxi. The bus probably left without us."

Asabi drew in another ragged breath and pulled Temly closer. She explained her plan. Temly nodded. "I understand. Leaving sounds fair."

"I can't—don't want to come to school today. I just want to gather my thoughts." Asabi moistened her lips. "So, you just go on, okay?"

"Sure. See you later."

Asabi nodded and waved her off. Temly stopped at the door to say something, but Asabi sat staring out the window just as she had moments before. Temly felt her friend's pain on a new level and swore to help.

She walked out of the house, running her hand over the textured surface of the walls, ruminating over her discussion with Asabi. Her heart raced in fear and excitement. "It is a good plan," she murmured.

As expected, the bus had left, so she waited by the road until a taxi approached. She waved it down and negotiated the fare. One of the two men in the taxi sat in front with the driver, while the other sat alone at the back. Temly joined the man in the back with a soft greeting. The man mumbled a response. She hoped she would get to school before the assembly in the school hall was over. Her school treated tardiness as a serious offence, and Temly would rather avoid discipline today.

A few meters down the road, the taxi driver stopped to pick a pregnant woman. The man beside the driver got into the back of the taxi with Temly and the other man to allow the pregnant woman to sit in front.

The man pushed Temly in and squeezed her against the other man. She started to protest, but the strange look in his dark eyes made her shudder. A sneer etched his face.

"This one will bring a good price."

Chapter Four

Asabi pulled off her socks and flexed her toes.

Slowly, she undressed and folded her uniform into a small traveler's bag from her closet. She didn't know if she'd ever need it, but there was no harm taking it. Besides, she liked the fabric and style and amused herself with thoughts of wearing it to remember her life here. Absurd, because nothing about what she had at the moment was worth a memorial. She should travel light. The bulk of her possessions were in her wallet—her debit card and international passport.

She stretched out on her bed and closed her eyes. Temly was so crucial to this plan, her visa to freedom, and she could only wait for her best friend to return from school. The plan was simple, and her friend would help.

The air-conditioning chilled the room, raising goose bumps all over her. Some days she thought she was beyond feeling anything. Especially those days. She counted her freedom in hours now. Freedom she had craved all her life. She had replied to the message from her father.

"I'm coming tomorrow." And he had sent an address—a popular fast-food restaurant in the Ikeja area of Lagos. She thought it was a most noble thing to do, to make their first meeting in a public place. Temly had bought the idea of leaving ASAP. Since Asabi didn't feel up to school, they'd agreed the plan would have to wait one more day.

The door opened, and Asabi jumped, grasping a blanket over her near nakedness. It was Missis, the housekeeper, with a mop and bucket and other cleaning paraphernalia. Missis yelped and clutched her throat.

"What are you doing here?"

Asabi dropped back on her bed and covered her body. Missis, a rotund, middle-aged woman, had been cleaning for Femi Fillips before Eni, Asabi's mother, married him. If she didn't know what had been going on in the house, then she was deaf, dumb, daft, and blind. She didn't deserve any respect.

Missis closed the door and dropped her cleaning materials. "Am I not talking to you?"

"I didn't go to school. I'm sick," Asabi said.

She drew the curtain back. Sunshine streamed in. It was nearly noon. Missis walked to the foot of Asabi's bed and pulled the blanket off her.

"*Come on* stand up and—"

Asabi lunged for the blanket before Missis could finish speaking. She twisted it from her hand and pushed her, causing the plump woman to stagger and fall.

"I'm sorry." Asabi's face crumbled, and tears dripped down her cheeks. When had she become this violent person?

Missis picked up her cleaning supplies and limped toward the door, closing it after her.

Asabi's hands trembled. The blanket she'd fought for lay on the floor. She stumbled to the window and closed the curtains. She couldn't take it anymore. Her stomach churned, and her silent tears became loud sobs. No more.

The walls of the house were thin, and she guessed the servants heard, but she couldn't care less. Today was the last day. Tomorrow she'd pick up the pieces of her life and move on.

Thoughts of what she needed to do flooded her mind. It was a plunge, moving from the known to the unknown, but she was ready. Clenching her jaw, she finished packing. Years of suffering had finally firmed what she planned today.

She wished her scheme offered more comfort, even with Temly aware of everything. But fear threatened her resolve. The uncertainty of the future caused her to pause a moment. Her heart pounded with the "what ifs." If anything went wrong, she would run to Temly's family. They'd been her rock the past ten years.

What if Temly changed her mind about helping? What if the plan didn't go as she hoped?

She dozed off as thoughts of freedom flooded her mind. She dreamed her birth father hugged her and welcomed her into a home more beautiful than anything Femi Filips could ever offer.

Someone patted her cheeks, and her eyes fluttered open.

Femi Filips' face came into focus. She stilled inside, her defense against his abuse. Beneath the blanket, she wore only her underwear. She shuddered at the consequences of what this meant.

Asabi stared at the face she hated most on earth. He rubbed her cheek with his thumb. She shrank from his touch. *Animal*, she thought. Her mother believed he was the most handsome of all beasts. Did her mother know the truth and ignore it?

"I heard you crying," he said softly.

His eyes roamed her face, gentle, searching, almost worried. But she saw beneath his tender words and looks. He violated her in the worst way possible.

He smoothed back her hair. "Why? Did I hurt you this morning?"

She clenched her teeth. She had resolved long ago not to say much when he was with her.

"You know how I want you. Sometimes I'm not patient. I don't mean to hurt you." He cupped her cheeks and bid her to look at him. "I never want to hurt you."

Her lids faltered. Anything to avoid a direct gaze. She found her voice, though it was thin with fright. "Where's my mom?"

"She's gone out. To work." He cleared his throat. "I know you're worried about her." He sighed. "But she's not a problem. All we need is three more years. Once you're old enough, I will divorce her. All she wants is money, and I'll give her whatever she wants." He winked. "Then I can marry you."

She swallowed and fought the urge to tell him where to go. The basest and hottest part of Hell. To let him know she wasn't marrying him when she was eighteen or ever. She wanted to laugh because she'd soon be free. He would never touch her again. He was a madman. But she closed her eyes instead, and tears flowed without warning.

"Why do you do this to me?" she whispered. At times, she wished she could kill him.

"I married your mom to be close to you." He cleaned her tears. "I fell in love with you the first day I saw you. Remember? You and Temly came to my pharmacy. I was fortunate to be there at the time because I don't visit often. You refused to take anything from me, though I offered to pay for your medication. Cough drops. Remember?" He chuckled.

She held her breath and willed strength.

"You were the most adorable thing I'd ever seen in my life. You wore a short, flared skirt with a denim jacket. Remember?"

She did. How could she not? In the last five years, he had reminded her of the evil day too many times. She remembered every detail, what was done, worn, and said.

"Please. Go."

He stood from the bed. "I'll send Missis to take care of you."

She breathed out. "No, I'm fine." She wanted to wipe her eyes but if she did, she would expose more than her head. She needed her arms to protect her more. "I am."

He walked to the door. "If you were fine, you'd be in school. I'll check back once Missis finishes taking care of you."

She threw on her jeans and a T-shirt the moment he left. She would get away from him today, and he'd never come near her again.

Chapter Five

Temly slowly climbed from blackness to a pungent taste in her mouth that reminded her of ammonium acid in the chemistry laboratory next to her class. She opened her eyes to another kind of darkness, a dead weight on her left shoulder.

She pushed herself up to shrug off a sleeping man's head and realized her hands were shackled. Her feet, too. From the hum of an engine, an uneven sway, and movements of bodies around her, she assumed she was in a truck—an open, moving truck packed full of people. The biting stench of urine accosted her, and she straightened as much as she could. A branch of leaves whipped her face and burned her eyes. She squinted. Nowhere to hide. A surge of nausea rose from her belly. *Oh* dear, why was she here?

A jolt lifted the truck off the road, and for a split second, cleared her mind.

Where am I? She peeked through and saw—nothing.

Her heart thudded. Dizzy from thirst, she fought to stay alert, hoping to see something, note landmarks, but everywhere was dark except for the space illuminated by the headlights of the vehicle. Another branch lashed her cheek, and she gave up seeking landmarks.

Desperate for water, she thought of the bottle in her school bag and moved for it, despite her restraints, but her hand touched someone who slapped it away.

She gasped. She'd been kidnapped!

The taxi man, the co-passenger's strange look and comment before he touched a kerchief to her face, and she blacked out. She tried to scream, but no sound came.

She told herself, *Calm down. Think.*

Dad said she was bright, and she must believe it. She closed her eyes. A woman beside her screamed. For the next few moments, chaos erupted as one by one others in the truck surfaced from their stupor. Chained hands slapped Temly's face from both sides as people groped in the dark, searching for a way out. She covered her head with her arms to block them as much as she could.

The truck jerked to a standstill, and she lifted her head with caution, fearful of being hit by man or plant. Terror clogged her chest.

With the headlights of the truck still on, she realized they were on a grassy space in the middle of nowhere. The little illumination helped her see the people around her.

A fresh bout of fear plummeted her stomach to the floor. Would her heart burst through her chest? Men lamented. Women cried. Little children wailed for their mothers. A pregnant woman wept—the same one who'd entered the taxi. Temly moved to comfort her, but she moaned in a strange language.

Fellow captives shouted as four men carrying weapons approached the truck—hefty, dark-skinned, with squared jaws and tight lips. Their unbuttoned shirts displayed sweaty, muscled chests, and their khaki shorts were stained with dark brown blotches shaped like hungry vultures.

The group of captives crouched together, the men pushing the women and children into a tight circle.

The men approached the truck from both ends, and two of them unlocked the catch of the trunk. With a slight tug on a long chain used to link the captives, the first man fell out of the truck, scattering the men's feeble attempt to protect the women and children.

One after the other, people fell out on wobbly legs, further complicated by their restraints.

The men surrounded the group, poking the male captives with the tips of their machetes.

"Ten. Complete," one said in a voice as rough as his looks.

Another one tugged on the end of their restraint, forcing the prisoners into a line. "Walk and do not utter a sound."

She'd heard stories of slave trading. It was a living nightmare. Now it seemed she was part of it.

No one protested. The pregnant woman sobbed, her clothes drenched in sweat. Another young lady cried out. One of the bare-chested men hit her face. She slumped, dragging a young boy in front of her down with her. His legs tangled with the pregnant woman who was in front of him. She shrieked as she resisted a fall and barely won.

This disrupted the line, and the captors stomped to the commotion, yelling. The one who'd hit the lady got into the line, unchained her from the group, removed her limp body, and swung her onto his shoulder. Another one lifted the boy and reattached the chains. The line continued to move.

The man took big strides with the woman. The truck's engine roared, and the driver revved it. Temly longingly watched as it was driven away, wondering if this was her last hope of leaving this nightmare. The man behind her pushed. She stumbled forward and mouthed a silent protest.

She wished she could rub her arms from the cold. The trek seemed unending, hypnotizing her. She thought of Mom, Dad, her brothers. And Asabi. Would she ever see them again?

The group burst out of the thick forest to an evening with moonlight, which made it possible to notice what resembled a small market in the middle of nowhere. Empty thatched kiosks contained only rafter benches and baskets. Temly's legs grew heavy, but the line kept moving, and she feared stopping.

Soon they left the clearing and entered a forest so dense the man in front used a machete to clear the way. Guards escorted them at the front and back. The man with the woman had disappeared.

Everyone continued in a noiseless parade sometimes broken with intermittent sobs and cries, which punctuated the cool night air. By now, Temly's legs were so heavy she didn't see how she could move another step, and yet she did. The group seemed to move as one.

Suddenly, she realized they had reached a settlement with pockets of lanterns in small huts. When had they arrived? The light from the huts spilled over a field-like arena.

The chains were loosed. Dumb-like, they were led to dwarf stakes and ordered to kneel, their hands tied behind their backs.

The cool grass beneath Temly offered little comfort to her tired legs. She would do anything for a sip of water. Maybe then she could talk. She tried to acquaint herself with her new environment by feeling. Nothing was familiar. Her bones felt weak.

What would happen now? What would everyone think? She'd run away? Her mother would be sick with worry. Her father would be angry. And Asabi— *Oh*, poor Asabi. Would she be able to follow through with her plan?

Time passed, impossible to measure. Tears trickled down her face again. She was so tired, weak, and hungry. She wished for sleep, wanted to wake up from this terrifying dream and discover she'd dozed off on her way to school.

Vibrations on the ground alerted her to guards walking along the stakes. One of two men yanked the small boy out of his restraints and flung him over his shoulder. The boy was limp as though dead. He must have fainted. Temly's gaze followed them until they entered some bushes. She didn't understand what this meant, and the bushes obscured her view.

The other guard came to her and loosed her bindings. With one hand, he lifted her to his shoulder and, much like the first had done with the boy, walked away.

Temly closed her eyes, her heart pounding harder than before. She hurt, ached for what she feared was ahead. She could think of nothing but the worst—rape, then death. She had no survivor skills. She had no strength to struggle. What would this achieve, anyway? Asabi had been through so much abuse, yet she never fought back. Temly could learn nothing from her experience.

The man took her to a brightly lit, empty mudroom and dropped her like a bean sack. She hit the hard floor on her back and moaned on impact. The light from a halogen bulb shone directly into her eyes. It occurred to her they had electricity. Or was this a generator? Whatever the case, this was not just a random location. It was a planned destination. The realization further dimmed her hope of escape.

The man tore her blouse, and she burst into tears. "Please. Don't."

Temly felt sick. She knew what was coming.

All of a sudden, her captor slapped her hard. Why? Her tongue seemed glued to the roof of her mouth. Would he beat her up before he violated her? Inflict pain, not because she struggled but out of plain wickedness? The only sound she could make came out like a squeak from a mouse. The angry man stomped out of the lighted room, leaving her shivering from head to toe.

He soon returned with another man, and Temly had no idea how she didn't die from fear. Two of them? They mumbled to each other, but she heard them clearly. Their words resounded in her ears. She wasn't good enough. They couldn't use her yet.

Once they left, she touched herself and confirmed their conversation. Her period had started. She didn't know whether to cry or be glad since it upset her captor. This should make her glad. It seemed he was not able to do what he wanted. It meant she was saved at least for a few days, if she didn't die of fear and hunger first.

Nausea rolled over her, and it hurt to breathe. Left alone for what seemed like forever, she fell into a coma-like sleep.

When she woke, she was back tied to the stake, doubled over. She peeked here and there, lethargic. Every muscle in her body quivered, and she wondered how much longer her physical strength would hold her. Her whole body burned. Her clothes were gone.

Naked and afraid, she wished for death. This nightmare had gone on for too long. Dawn seemed to break, and the early morning dew chilled her.

Chapter Six

Asabi checked her watch.

Temly ought to be back from school. Where was she? If she'd come as agreed, they'd probably be in her house now, tidying up the plans to disappear forever, to a place only her friend knew of.

Asabi's stomach twisted. In one breath, she was angry and in the next, afraid. She needed Temly to help her vanish. Had her friend pulled out at the last minute? Or had she shared the problem with her mother? No mother would ever agree to such a plan.

Her phone rang, and she snatched it, hoping it was her friend. It was Temly's mother.

"Hello, dear. Is Temly with you?"

"No, ma'am."

"Do you know where she might be?"

It took a moment before Asabi understood the question. If Temly wasn't at home, where was she?

"No." Asabi sat up. Where had she gone? She was supposed to come here. "Maybe the bus was delayed a bit or something." But the bus was never late.

Temly's mother sighed. "I'll call the school and find out." She ended the call.

Asabi checked the time again. Eighteen hours. A lump in her throat grew. She paced the floor and caught her image in the full-length mirror.

She'd carefully chosen her outfit: a sleeveless floral dress, with a black boyfriend jacket and black sandals. She came across as innocent, harmless. No one would suspect she was on the run. She was just a nice girl on an errand for her mother at the grocery store.

She cupped her cheeks. Where had Temly gone? They were meant to go to her house together and pretend to leave for the grocery store down the road. From there, Asabi was to pick up her traveling bag, which ought to have been dropped before getting to Temly's, and get a taxi to the bus station, from where she would go to Lagos. It was a perfect plan. Temly would wait two hours, confirm she was in Lagos, and then tell her mother.

Asabi called Mel, who though was her presumed enemy, had information on everyone in the class. Mel had not seen Temly in school. Mel started to say something about Romeo, the supposed lover Asabi wanted to snatch, but she cut the line.

She leaned back and stared into space. Temly was missing! If she'd left her house and didn't get to school… The thought of what could have happened made her sick. An accident? She had to go find her.

Asabi didn't have to tell anyone where she was off to. They didn't care. Her home wasn't like Temly's where everyone loved and respected one another. Here, no one did.

She chose the kitchen exit, sure Missis would be the only one there, and it wouldn't matter if she answered the older woman's questions or not.

Her mother was at the sink when Asabi stepped in. She scowled. "I didn't know you came in from school."

Asabi swallowed. "Yes. Not long ago."

Her mother's pretense had only grown worse, and Asabi doubted her ability to continue holding up the fake relationship between them.

"How was school?"

"Fine."

Asabi headed for the door. Better to take the front door since her mother was here.

"You didn't go to school today. Asabi, when will you stop lying?"

Asabi stopped short, her hand already on the door handle. She took two deep breaths and faced Eni. "I went to school." She snickered. "But you never notice."

The look on her mother's face confirmed Asabi's thoughts. "Who do you think you're talking to?"

Asabi took a deep breath. "I'm sorry, Mom."

She left the kitchen. Femi Filips was in the living room, reading. Asabi stiffened and walked to the front door and didn't stop, even when Femi called to ask where she was off to.

She took a taxi to Temly's house.

The calm outside mirrored none of the chaos Asabi met inside. Bola Cole, Temly's mother, rushed to her. Her father, Kenny Cole's face was creased with age lines Asabi had never noticed before, and Temly's two older brothers, Tayo and Tunji, sat mute.

"*Ah* Asabi, I'm glad you're here. The school matron said Temly wasn't in school at all today! Did you see her? Why didn't you tell us she hadn't gone to school?"

Asabi trembled. "I didn't go either."

All eyes focused on her. Without intending to, she broke down and cried.

Chapter Seven

Asabi explained Temly's visit but omitted why she hadn't gone to school. A part of her wanted to tell Bola Cole, but she was afraid they wouldn't believe her.

"You're saying Temly left your house and said she was going to school?" Mr. Cole said.

"Yes, sir. But the bus had left by then, so she must have taken a taxi."

"Do you know which one?" he said.

"No, sir." Asabi swallowed a lump in her throat. For the first time, she was afraid for Temly. The anger had gone. Where was she?

The Cole family was large, and with Mr. Cole's twin brother being the governor of the state, there were many friends to call. He grabbed his phone and left the room.

Mrs. Cole paced. Tunji and Tayo leaned against the walls, a frown on each of their faces. Temly had been so attached to her brothers. Asabi studied the boys' profiles. They all, including Temly, had their father's dark complexion and their mom's oblong-shaped face and eyes. Otherwise, the Cole children bore a resemblance to one another but nothing to their parents.

Asabi's heart beat rapidly. *Temly, where are you?*

Mr. Cole walked in a few minutes later. "Tai's sending two police officers from the governor's lodge to the house."

"Did she say anything about what she wanted to do, anywhere she wanted to go?" Mrs. Cole asked for the umpteenth time.

Asabi shook her head. "Just that she'd check on me after school."

"But why didn't you go to school? The matron said she didn't receive a call from your parents."

"Because—we thought—"

Mrs. Cole's voice was high-pitched. "*Oh* my! Since morning and no one called to say anything. Why didn't you call us when you didn't see her after school? What if I didn't call you to ask if she—"

"Honey, calm down." Mr. Cole patted his wife's back. "Temly will be home soon. We have to believe she's okay."

Mrs. Cole dropped onto the couch beside Asabi. Her tears mingled with Asabi's, punctuated by Mr. Cole's calls to friends and family.

Mrs. Cole squinted at her husband. "Maybe you should stop calling people. Alarming others when she could be fine or could—or do we need to raise an alarm, because Temly has always been responsible?"

Asabi tried to think of ways to help. "Our security man could have seen the taxi Temly got into."

Mrs. Cole startled. "Yes. We have to talk to him."

Mr. Cole mumbled to Asabi, "Honey, don't you think we should call your parents before we question the security man?"

"It's not necessary."

He shook his head. "What were you girls doing when you were supposed to be on the bus?"

Asabi wrung her hands. The truth would only cause more trouble. If she'd been outside her gate and ready to get on the bus, nothing would have happened. "This is all my fault."

"Of course not." Mrs. Cole's voice softened. "It's getting late anyway, and I think we should notify your parents about what's going on."

The police officers from the governor's office arrived and questioned Asabi and members of the family. When they learned Asabi was the last to see Temly, they drilled her again.

Then they proceeded to search the house.

Mr. and Mrs. Cole sat in the kitchen. Tunji followed the police officers to Temly's room while they searched for anything that could lead them to her location. Temly was painfully organized and happy with her life. From all indications, she had no reason to disappear. The men returned to the kitchen with her iPad and a school notebook.

Mrs. Cole stood. "Anything?"

The first officer, a tall, slender, dark-skinned, middle-aged man, with dark, intelligent eyes, took a deep breath. "We need to take these with us to the station. Can you give us her password?"

Mrs. Cole sighed. "I don't know." She faced Asabi. "Do you have it?"

Asabi nodded. The shorter, thickset second officer, who seemed much younger, gave her a piece of paper and pen, and she scribbled down the password. "She uses the same password for all her social media pages and chat groups."

The officer nodded. "We have her cell phone. Asabi, we'd like for you to come with us to the station."

Mr. Cole stepped in front of her. "No. Her parents have to give their consent."

His protective gesture was not lost on Asabi. Her mom never took her side on anything, and Femi Filips had only his selfish interest in her. But she was too consumed with the tragedy of the moment to acknowledge the gesture she never found at home. "I don't mind. Just Temly—she should be found." A long sob escaped. She couldn't help it.

Tunji, the older of Temly's brothers drew her close.

"Her parents have to know she's going to the police station," Mr. Cole said. "I won't allow her to go alone."

The officer nodded. "Can you give us her parents' numbers? We will call and—"

"No, don't call them, please." Asabi tapped Mrs. Cole. "Ma'am, can you come with me?"

"But they'll be worried."

"No, they won't be." She nearly added 'they don't care,' but didn't. Not here. Not now.

"We need to have your statement at the station, too," the officer said to Mr. Cole.

"We'll go together then." Mrs. Cole picked her two cell phones. She sniffed. "If anyone calls—"

"We're coming with you, too," Tunji said.

"No. She may come home—" Mrs. Cole bit her lower lip to stop her tears.

Her husband drew her into his arms. "Temilola'll be fine. We have to believe it."

Tayo's stone-cold profile crumbled, and he wept.

Chapter Eight

Asabi sat with her hands clasped on her lap, her back straight.

Mrs. Filips paced and punctuated harsh words with hisses. "You always feel you know best. You want to disgrace the family and us. *Hmm*? And you sat in your room, pretending to be sick. Stupid girl—"

"Mrs. Filips, please," Mr. Cole said.

"No, let me talk to her. I mean, what kind of thing is this? And she just walked out of the house. No regard for anybody!" She confronted Asabi. "I won't let you send me to an early grave by your actions. Do you understand?"

"We are at least grateful Wale got a good description of the taxi Temly got into. I'm sure the taxi drivers' association will be able to identify the driver," Femi said softly.

"The school has launched a campaign, too." Mrs. Cole sighed. "Thanks so much for your help. And support."

Mr. Cole nodded. "I'm sure they'll find her. She'll be fine."

Femi Filips patted Mrs. Cole's hand. "I can't imagine how this must be for you—"

Mrs. Filips smirked at her husband's comment in her usual antagonistic way. "Don't you have anything else to say?" She touched Mrs. Cole's hand, too. "I'm sure this must be tough."

Femi nodded. "We will do everything we can. I will personally follow up with Wale and the taxi drivers' association."

Mr. and Mrs. Cole stood. Femi stood, too. As did Asabi.

"I'm going to stay at Temly's house till she's found," Asabi said.

Mrs. Filips gasped. "You don't even feel any remorse for your part in all this?" She addressed Mrs. Cole. "You see what I'm talking about? She thinks she's the queen of the world—you're not going anywhere."

Asabi walked toward her room, ignoring her mother's demands.

Femi sighed. "I'll talk to her."

Asabi heard the Coles' discussion with her mother, but she didn't care about what they had to say. She entered her room and walked to her dresser. She'd planned to move to Temly's house anyway, to her safe haven. This just made things a little easier.

When she walked out of this house, she would never come back. She removed her small traveling bag from her closet. Most of her clothes would be left behind, but it mattered little, since Femi Filips bought them all. With her father, she would get new ones.

"Don't move to the Coles' house," Femi said.

Asabi stilled. She hadn't heard him walk in. He stood so close to her, if she moved, she'd fall into his arms.

He breathed down her neck. "I can't stay here without you."

Asabi lowered her voice. "If you don't get away from me, I'm going to scream so loud, the Coles will think I found Temly's dead body in my closet."

Femi stepped back. "You're trying to intimidate me."

Asabi carried her bag to her bed and opened it. Everything remained.

"Don't leave me."

She straightened, lifted the small luggage and her school bag, and checked around the room. For the last time.

"You look so beautiful."

Asabi walked to the door. He pinned her to the wall and pressed a long kiss to the curve of her shoulder and neck.

"I love you so much, Asabi. Don't leave me with your mother. Please." He pressed small kisses on her shoulder. "Please, my love."

He brought her to face him and cupped her cheeks. "My love. Sweet love."

Asabi stifled a scream and pushed back with all her strength. She whirled and bumped into her mother.

"Mom!"

Eni Filips raised her hand to slap her, but Femi caught it just in time.

Her face twisted with hatred, and Asabi didn't think any evil stepmother could have beaten her at meanness.

"You little witch, seducing my husband all these years."

She pressed her lips together and fought tears. No, she would not let the woman who birthed her see how much she hurt.

Femi released her hand with force, and she staggered back. "You are the evil one, and you've always known it."

Asabi ran out of the room with her bags and a silent vow to never return.

Chapter Nine

"Where did they take you?"

Temly arched her neck toward the whispered words. The speaker was the pregnant woman. No one else was at their stakes. A full moon shone high in the sky, bright and illuminating their surroundings. She could see as clear as day and wondered what time it was. There was darkness beyond, where the settlement ended, and the jungle began.

"Where is everybody?" the woman said. "They just keep taking people, one by one."

Temly didn't know what had happened to the others. *Lord, I don't want to die.* She repeated it several times in her fear.

She stared at the pregnant woman again. The woman returned her gaze.

"Please, ma'am," she said. Tears clogged her throat, and her head began to throb. "Please ma'am, where are we? What happened to us?"

"This is an evil forest, but God will fight for me." The woman spoke through a ragged voice.

Her words stung Temly, whose lips trembled, and tears came down in torrents. She believed God would hear the prayers. *What about me? Would God save only one person?*

"*Shh*. Stop crying. Stop crying."

The urgency in the woman's voice halted her tears. She blinked and hiccupped.

"Where did they take you?"

Temly sniffed and focused on her. "*Huh*?"

"They took you away. People taken away were not brought back. Only you. Where did they take you to?"

"I don't know—"

"You don't know?"

"I—he—"

"Only you and I are left here. When they take someone, they don't bring them back. No one has come for me." She sounded impatient, as though the information was pertinent to the success of a plan. "So, what happened to you? Where did they take you?"

Temly dropped her head.

The woman's voice rose. "And then brought you back again?"

Temly processed the question. "A room." Recalling the ordeal made her shiver. She lowered her voice to a whisper. "He touched me, and then, and then—"

"And then?"

Temly blinked tears away. "Inside—my—" She inspected her legs as though a third had grown.

"Don't say it! Fire on him. Fire on them."

There was another chilled silence between them, and the curious lady drew a deep breath. "You were violated?"

"*Umm*, my monthly started." Goosebumps rose on her arms. "It hadn't started before—I mean, it's not due. I don't know why now." She couldn't believe she could mutter these words to a total stranger. Talking about this with her mother had always made her uneasy.

"How did you know?"

"He touched me—there." She sobbed. "He was angry. He slapped me and left me." She inhaled. "Then he came back with another man, and they talked about it. The other one said it was a taboo, or something similar. I pretended I didn't hear them."

The pregnant woman shushed her again. "When they brought you in, you were unconscious." She lowered her voice. "I thought they would take me, and I started to fire prayers. Then God heard my cry and they left. Maybe they don't want someone having her period. Or a pregnant one."

"I hope they kill me instead."

"Don't talk so. Don't you believe in God? Don't you go to church?"

"We go. Sometimes."

Now she couldn't control her tears. These horrible men would not take her home. She would die here, unless this was slave trading. Why had her monthly come early? What did this mean?

"Stop crying, girl. Can't you pray instead?" The woman muttered words Temly couldn't comprehend.

Temly sniffed. "Where are you from?"

She frowned. "Why do you ask?"

"I have never heard this language before."

"It's not a language. It is called tongues."

Temly leaned closer to get a better view of the woman. Her stomach was huge. She had a fair, pretty face and smooth skin.

"Don't tell me you have never heard of speaking in tongues before?"

"I don't think I have. It sounds odd." Temly wished she could blow her nose and clean her face, but her hands remained tied behind her back.

"It's strange, but it is the one thing we need for our salvation from here."

"Please teach me how to speak."

She considered Temly with all seriousness. "Repeat after me." She went ahead and combined several syllables. Temly repeated them as best as she could.

"What does it mean?"

"It is God's language, a prayer."

For the next few minutes, Temly learned the spiritual language, believing it would save her body and soul. Then they both prayed it. Over and over again they chanted.

The day finally dawned. Three mud huts surrounded a small clearing. The two captives were tied to two stakes behind them. Temly guessed she'd been taken to one of the huts to be examined. Several other stakes were empty and surrounded the huts. What had happened to the other people?

The landscape showed level, grassy ground spanned over an extensive radius. How could they escape without being seen?

"What's your name?" Her fellow hostage's voice came to Temly from a distance.

She jolted and swallowed. "Temilola Cole—Temly."

"How old are you?"

"Fifteen."

"The God I serve will take us away from this place. I am convinced in my spirit."

They both sat quietly for a long time. Temly was lost in her thoughts. Her stomach rumbled, and she wished she'd eaten breakfast like her mother always quarreled with her to do—though this would have made little difference two days later.

To be hungry under such a terrifying circumstance was amazing. Temly thought fear and danger could chase hunger away. She didn't want to die. She wanted her mother so much, yet she couldn't make herself think about home or the good things or people she would rather be with.

No, she couldn't think of home. "What's your name, ma'am?"

"Martha." Her head drooped. "Please be strong. God will deliver us from here."

As the day wore on worry, muscle pain, and hunger welcomed dusk. The second day was fading away and there was nothing Temly could do. Her hands were tied so tight it was impossible to shift them. They'd neither seen nor heard anyone.

She observed Martha, whose head had fallen on her chest. Temly tried to speak the language she had taught her but to no avail. She couldn't remember the words.

"*Oh* God, help me. Help both of us, God."

She hoped the spiritual language would come back to her. As darkness closed in, a new fear gripped her. How was she going to clean up with her period in this situation? How was she going to survive another night without food or water? Naked and cold. And what would happen tomorrow?

"Aunty Martha, I don't know what to do," she said to the night sky. "Aunty Martha?" She called out when she heard no response. "Aunty Martha?"

"The God of Elijah and the God of Pastor Favor will not let us down," came a weak voice from the dark. It did not resemble the voice of the convincing woman who had spoken with so much assurance earlier.

"Pastor Favor?"

"Pastor Favor Peter. He's my father in the Lord." Her voice rose. "I have been praying to God in his name all day, and rescue is sure. You just hold on." Her voice faded. But in the silence surrounding them, Temly heard, "He is our only hope. His God is our only help."

Temly pondered on her words. She wanted to be sure of her fate. She wondered why Martha would pray in a man's name, and not God's or Jesus's.

"He will send help. I have spoken the words of truth. It will come. Sleep, dear child. Tomorrow and our salvation dawns soon. Pastor Favor always comes through."

"Amen," Temly whispered.

Her eyelids drooped, and her tongue scrolled across her cracked lips. The cold night raised more fear for tomorrow.

One of the men appeared. Temly closed her eyes and remained still—ready to be taken again. The man held a bright lantern in one hand that lit up the whole area, and a carved knife in the other. He walked to Martha and cut her loose. Temly heard no protest and thought Martha might be asleep.

She heard voices and opened her eyes slightly, afraid she'd be noticed.

A well-dressed man walked behind the evil captor who said, "We got new intakes. You'll be pleased."

"This time, I hope we have a two-in-one. I don't want to make mistakes like the last time."

The abductor nodded and nudged Martha. The other man placed a ringed finger on her swollen belly. Her eyes widened at the man and she mumbled, "Pastor Favor. You came. I knew you would come."

The man staggered back as though he'd been struck and rushed away. Martha pressed her lips together, and her face relaxed. Temly's heart thudded. Why would a pastor come here? How had Martha known he would, in the middle of nowhere? Her skin crawled with jealousy. Who would come and save her?

But when the captor examined Martha, there was menace in his gaze. He threw her over his shoulder in much the same way Temly had been taken the day before, and Martha's arms dangled behind him. Maybe the pastor's touch had killed her. Maybe God had taken her to save her from the pain of death. Or did she faint from joy?

Temly was alone now. When the retreating lantern closed darkness around her, she screamed.

A hand clamped over her mouth, a mouthful of words pierced through her marrow.

"Shut up. Or do you want to die?"

Chapter Ten

Temly struggled to breathe, but the hand over her mouth stopped her screaming. His words reverberated in her brain. *Shut up! Or do you want to die? Do you want to die—? Do you want to die—die—die—?*

He loosed the rope binding her hands, though his hand over her mouth never lost its grip. She closed her eyes, wishing this away, all of it. But if this were a nightmare, it had gone on for too long.

Temly couldn't think while the hand was over her mouth, only obey the voice. He lifted her and dragged her back over the hard clay ground. She wanted to fight him but couldn't. Maybe he knew she was too weak.

After a while, he stopped. "You need to walk. Can you?" His voice was soft. Soothing. Was he an angel of God or what?

Temly tried to speak, but her throat was dry. She tried again and a rasp came from deep within her belly.

He breathed hard and released her. She twisted to face him and opened her eyes, unsure, afraid of what she would see.

They were not anywhere close to where she'd been tied. With thick darkness all around, she couldn't see his face.

"You need to be able to walk."

Temly shook her head because it was all she had strength to do. He protested softly and carried her much like a baby, cradled in his arms.

He seemed to know his way, and soon they arrived at a clearing about the size of her standard parlor at home. It was obvious someone had done some crude grass cutting and scraping because the vegetation beyond the area was wild. He gently let her down, and she fought tears. He had a small lantern, which only illuminated the immediate space and a shadow of the bordering thick forest.

"You need water?"

She nodded. What a question! She wanted to scream, beg, die—for water.

He put a bottle to her lips, and she drank greedily. The water ran a chilling course down her throat to her belly, reminding her of her nakedness. She covered her chest with feeble hands, but when he lowered the mouth of the bottle, she let go of her cover and gripped his hand with both of hers. Her fear escalated.

He didn't move. When she thought she'd had enough water, she released him and attempted to cover herself.

"Where am I? Who are you?" Temly said softly, catching her first real glimpse of him.

He had long hair, plaited back in cornrows. He was slim, and most likely cream-colored in better light. Tall too, and young. Not a full-grown man, but with strong arms.

"It's a long story. And I would love to hear yours, too." He sat opposite her and folded his arms across his chest.

"But—" She wanted to stop the tears.

He held up his hand. "I know this is hard, but I would like to know." He put the bottle to his mouth. After a quick swig, he lowered it and assessed her.

She stared back and shivered, not just from cold. They were in the middle of nowhere, and his eyes devoured her like she was food for a hungry man. If only she had something to cover her nakedness. She didn't know who he was. How did he get here? What could someone so young be doing in this thick bush? Was he an escapee?

Then she startled. He wore a long white robe. Like an angel. She was staring at a real angel. He'd saved her. She shuddered, and her eyes rolled back in their sockets.

A mix of emotions overwhelmed her. God had sent an angel to rescue her. It was too much. She collapsed, and the world went completely black.

****

Fela whirled around. Had she seen something? There was nothing unusual. He carried the girl and laid her under the tree. Whatever made her faint would not stop him from finding food. Yet, he couldn't leave her.

She was small and young. Judging from her size, she may be just a little older than his sister, Diamond, who was only ten years old. Poor soul.

As strange as it sounded, he still couldn't believe he had lost the path to get food at the regular place. But now he could see God wanted him to save the poor girl.

If only he'd gotten to the site a little earlier, he might have saved the pregnant woman, too. But how would he have helped a woman in her condition? At least he could help the girl.

But what would he do with her? He didn't even know how long he could survive in this wilderness, let alone now with this young girl who was weak, exhausted, and scared to death. And naked. How would he cope with her? He settled back to wait until she wakened then he'd figure out how to get food.

In the past two days, he'd seen the bush populated and depopulated. Like a market day ritual. One day, the place was full to the brim. The next, no one.

The girl stirred and whimpered, causing his attention to shift to her. Slowly, she sat and gauged her surroundings, disoriented. Then her gaze settled on him, and she scooted back. Her hand flew to her mouth and she stifled a scream.

He rubbed his chin. "I won't harm you."

"Are you an angel?"

Despite himself, Fela threw his head back and laughed, harder than three days ago when he and Law cracked some silly joke. So, she thought he was an angel?

It felt good, especially staring at her as she laughed until she cried.

He contemplated, unsure how to console her. They needed to find something to eat.

"Look—see we need to get food."

He pulled off the long white gown and handed it to her. It had played a significant role in him being alive, but the girl's nakedness embarrassed him as much as he was sure it did her.

"Here. Take." He held it out to her, and she reached out with shaky hands. "We need to get you covered. The insects here have spirit, soul, and body."

She slipped it over her head, reminding him of a cornered animal.

"Come," he stretched his hand to her, "I can't leave you here." She continued to whimper. He shrugged. "Well, stay then. But anything can happen while I'm gone. To me or you."

She failed to respond. Was this shock?

He lifted his T-shirt from a scrub and pulled it over his head with the hope he could get another gown like he got the first.

He headed in the opposite direction, believing she'd follow him. He guessed she would be too frightened left alone in the dark.

She wobbled after him. "Please, don't leave me."

He faced her. "What's your name?"

She blinked at him and shrugged.

"Well, it's not important, is it?" He continued to walk. He could feel her anxiety and ever-present fear.

This was a path he had come to know in the last couple of days. It was gruesome. He knew what to expect—he ought to prepare her. It was a long walk, but as they approached their destination, he spoke to her.

"You can wait here while I look for food."

She shook her head. "No. No."

"Calm down. Look, this is a wild for—"

"No."

"Listen to me, just like you, someone out there thinks I'm a ghost or something, and so they leave me alone and I can do what—"

"No. You can't leave me here."

"Look, we are in the middle of a shrine or something. There are killers. The people who captured you." He held her slim shoulders with both hands and shook her gently. "Stay here. I won't be long."

"What if—they see me?"

Her voice was so feeble; it tore at his heart. She was right. What if they saw her?

He bit his lower lip. "They'll think you're a ghost, too."

He couldn't tell her he risked being seen as an escaped captive without the gown, or that she would be dead if a wild animal got her. He hadn't been there long enough to comprehend what lived here.

"Come. Sway like a—like anything. And if I tell you to run, you run. Anything I tell you to do, just do it, okay?" He sighed. "Now, walk in front of me. Slowly."

She nodded and then moaned an okay.

"What's your name?"

"Temly."

"Walk in front. Follow the path."

Chapter Eleven

When Fela and Temly got to the altar where offerings of fruits, drinks, and clothing had been placed, two rough-looking men stood rooted to the ground, staring ahead with soulless eyes. Fela couldn't imagine how humans could become so gross, uncaring, and evil. What sort of existence did these men have? Were they mortal? They did resemble humans, but their actions were questionable.

The first time Fela saw them, he thought they'd kill him. He'd stood frozen, waiting, and when they fell on their faces, he had taken to his heels and run. When he realized they weren't following him, he'd watched for a long time to see what would happen. The men slowly stood, sneaked a quick look around, laughed, and ran in the opposite direction. Perhaps to relate their joy in seeing a 'deity' come to receive the sacrifice? He didn't get it.

They must have thought he was a god or something. Remembering brought a little smile to his face, but he knew they would scare Temly. He'd rushed back and stolen water and cooked food laid out on the wood. The rafter altar dripped with blood from the human head placed on it. These evil pictures were burned on his memory. But he had to live, one day at a time.

"Raise your hands," he said. "Pick up the food when they fall on their faces."

Temly obeyed. He raised his hands high in the air as well, and the two men fell to the ground. They took what they could carry and hurried away.

He imagined she'd be terrified, but she only clenched her arms by her side. She swallowed hard and picked up what she needed with swift, jerky movements. Perhaps she'd relive this experience and react later, but for now, she worked with a calculated frenzy.

Once they returned to the secluded area, she exploded in hysterical laughter. She continued until he worried she would hurt herself. And she didn't stop till they reached the clearing.

After carefully dropping the supplies, she slumped onto the ground and took huge gulps of air. He studied her, his head cocked to one side. Even in the middle of danger, she was intriguing. The strength and gait she used to carry all the stuff they stole made him think she must be strong, perhaps stronger than she realized.

She opened a can of cold malt drink and slugged it down so fast she spilled it on the front of the white gown. He picked another can and sipped a little. She slid back until she lay on her back and stared up in the sky.

"Sit up and let's eat," Fela said.

Everything was better now than when he was alone. Fear had stopped him from taking anything more than a bottle of water and a plate of food. This time, they'd stolen much more. Would the men be after them when they discovered the extent of their theft? He refused to think what they might do.

"Temly?" He checked her out in the dim light. "Come on." He chuckled. She was out. Fast asleep, with the can by her side.

He lowered his almost full drink and moved toward her.

He remembered what he'd seen before here. The other night, there were more fresh heads. He stumbled into an actual killing. She was lucky! He squeezed his eyes shut. Images of the strong man dropped on the floor and his head plucked off with a machete like a chicken's left his skin cold. It was grisly. Blood was everywhere.

He shook his head to clear it and carried her closer to the tree where he'd managed to make a bed of sorts from clothes he'd taken from rituals, bales of wax and white, red, and black cloths.

After his first encounter when the captors thought he was some sort of spirit, he'd tied pieces of white sheets, pulled off his t-shirt, and worn the makeshift robe over his jeans.

When he thought about it, he cringed. How else could he survive here? To be reduced to deceiving demons was more than he ever imagined in his wildest thoughts.

Earlier, he'd been too frightened to take much but tonight, Temly had acted bravely. She'd walked ahead of him to the altar, and for a moment, they both scanned the area for danger. The fresh head of the woman he'd seen earlier with her was on the altar. He knew because of the bloodied hair, but Temly either had a strong stomach or had blocked the horrific sight. He swiped at his eyes. He and Temly could be next.

He'd stolen a glance at the two men on their faces. Guards worshipping while the "spirits" fed on the sacrifice.

Temly didn't wait for him. She put a carton of biscuits on a carton of the malt drink and placed them all in a big basket of fruit. "Can you put this on my head?"

He did and was surprised at her balance. She must have been one of the girls who hawked on the streets.

He loaded himself, too, taking two cartons of water, a bale of wax material, a pot of cooked food, packets of sweets, and a big basket of fruits. He found a way to load them all.

They were panting when they cleared the ritual sites. He was proud of her. Now they had to think of how to leave this forest. At least they had enough food and water for a few days.

He opened the pot of food and found yam porridge. The same food he'd found the first time. Was it the food of the gods? He dug in, enjoying every bite of the well-seasoned food.

When he was full, he spread more bales of cloth on the ground and made another bed beside Temly. Then he snuggled up next to her and covered them both with the thick, red material. He drew in a sharp breath—red, the color of blood.

He fell asleep for the third night in the middle of nowhere with thoughts of what the forest represented and the hideous sacrifices. Poor, innocent people fallen into the hands of malicious men.

He thought of his father. What he must think about him now? He prayed he'd be saved from nightmares tonight.

Chapter Twelve

Temly awoke warm under the thick red cover.

It took her several moments to remember what had happened since she left Asabi. Fela's hot breath fanned her arm and helped to quicken her memory. Her heart thudded.

She let out a soft breath, and her stomach twisted with hunger. When was the last time she ate anything? She moaned, and Fela shifted.

He stretched. "*Wow*, what a night." He tossed off the blanket and stood. "The sun is up." He yawned. "You need to get up."

She'd slept close to a stranger. The thought made her blanch. She still sometimes slept in her brothers' beds, but this was different. She was unwilling to let him see her humiliation. She noticed the unique way the branches of the tree formed a roof over their heads. How could he know if the sun was up or not?

Temly sighed. "It must have been hard to find such a tree."

"Such a tree?" He followed her gaze. "I never noticed." He glanced at her. "No wonder I have to get on the path before I know if it's night or day."

"You never noticed?"

Fela chuckled. His Adam's apple bobbed up and down, and she couldn't guess his age. What was she going to do now? Stick with a total stranger? They had to find a way to escape.

Fela opened the pot of porridge and took a deep breath. The aroma of the food wafted to Temly and her stomach rumbled.

"If you take shelter in those bushes for privacy, you can use some of the water to clean up, and join me. The food tastes better than anything I ever had."

Temly remembered her monthly. "*Oh* my." She moaned.

Fela reacted. He dropped the cover of the pot and swung to her. "What?"

"*Ur*, sorry. I'm I—"

"You wet?"

Better than the truth, Temly thought. She considered the bushes. How was she going to take care of this?

"*Ah*. My sister still wets the bed and she's fourteen." Fela chuckled. "Go on, I'm not looking."

Temly wrapped the sheets around her and walked to the other side of the tree. She hated this time of the month. Yet it had saved her life. Fela had graciously left several bottles of water.

Temly cleaned herself and tore a piece of cloth, which she used as a pad. Then she washed her face and inside her mouth. She felt much better.

When she returned to Fela, he was eating.

"By noon, it will be sour, but we'll most likely get another pot in the night."

"I'm not going to be here in the night."

He stopped his hand halfway to his mouth. "How do you think you'll get out of here?"

"How do you think you can stay here with what we saw?" Temly sat opposite him and dipped her hand in the pot. "*Hmm*?"

Fela laughed. "The gods enjoy."

She peered at him. "Even in this thick forest, you crack jokes?"

"You thought I was an angel or a ghost. So," he shrugged. "It's funny."

They ate in silence. Temly opened a can of malt and drank it all in two gulps. Fela rested against the tree.

"I'm serious. I won't stay here," she said.

"I don't see what choice we have. We don't even know where on earth this is."

Temly bit the inside of her cheek. How did he get in the forest? Without doubt, he must see reason with her. They couldn't stay in this forest with the evil men.

"We need to find a way out. I want to go home." She belched and coughed.

She'd made a mistake drinking the hot malt too fast. She'd never been a fan of the rich drink like Asabi. But it was either the drink or water, and now water was more precious because of her condition.

Her heart throbbed at the possibilities they faced. Fela was right to conclude they had no choice. On the other hand, how long could they stay here in the forest? Feasting off the wicked fate of the others who weren't so lucky.

Temly swallowed hard. "You must have some plans, don't you? You must have people who would look for you?"

"Do you have people looking for you?"

She frowned for a moment. "Of course. I know my parents and my best friend will be searching."

Fela arched an eyebrow. "Where? Where do you think they'll look? Do you know how you got here?"

"I was in a taxi going to school—" She took in air and pressed her lips together.

He gave a curt nod. "My thoughts exactly."

"We must find a way out. I want to go home. I miss my home. I want my family." She swallowed so she wouldn't cry. "I'm not going back to see sacrifices of innocent people and play ghost games." She rubbed her throbbing forehead. "I'll go mad if I stay here. I want to go *home*. And I expect you do, too." She took a step backward when he didn't respond. "Do you have a home?"

"Yes."

"You don't seem eager to leave here."

Temly's heart skipped a beat at the lost look in his eyes. Could he be a ghost so comfortable in this forest? What would she do if he changed into a monster or something? Or walked into the forest and became a tree. Her imagination was going crazy. Maybe she was losing her mind.

She took a few steps back and clenched her fists. "You're not human?"

Chapter Thirteen

"Of course, I'm human." Fela heaved a heavy sigh. "I'm here because I followed my dad. He left me in the forest and drove off."

Temly shook her head. It was the craziest thing she'd ever heard. She needed to be sure she heard him right. "Your dad brought you here to sacrifice you?"

Fela lifted his chin. If he didn't want to talk, she could understand, but she had to know. He knew how she'd gotten here, or at least had an idea.

"I want to know what happened to you. I mean, I can't imagine why you or anyone at all would be living in the bush for—"

"I don't live in the bush." He threw his hands in the air and walked to the makeshift bed. With jerky movements, he folded it and packed the supplies together.

Temly moved closer to him. "What are you doing?"

"Getting ready to leave."

He kicked the near-empty pot of food into the bush and tore the carton of malt drinks, spilling the cans all over the ground. He kicked the tree and fell on his knee. He groaned, but not from pain. This was emotional.

Temly's hand trembled, but she touched his shoulder. "I'm sorry."

She picked up the cans of drinks and rolled them into a sheet. He needed time to work through whatever bothered him. His father must have hurt him, to say the least. Fela swiped at his eyes and joined her. In silence, they packed the drinks and biscuits into the bales of cloth, tying them as tightly as possible, and placed them on their heads.

Fela picked up a machete he'd found near the food and pointed toward the thick forest. "This way."

Temly's thoughts raced. *What's next, dear God of heaven? Whoever You are and wherever You live. What's next?*

She followed him though. The forest floor had shrubs of thick undergrowth and tall trees with fat trunks. Several times she feared animals would fall off the drooping branches. With no path to follow, they tripped over old stumps and unseen pebbles. She didn't think he knew his way, and it soon became obvious they needed to stop and strategize.

"Fela. Fela." Temly struggled to breathe. "I need to rest. Please."

He stopped walking, his face like stone. He breathed hard as well. He helped her to put down the wrap on her head and dropped his, too. They sat on the ground, and they stretched aching necks and shoulder muscles.

Her feet bled from tripping over stumps. She blinked back tears. "If only we knew the time."

"I have a watch." Fela pulled out a wristwatch from his pocket and checked it. "It's a quarter to three."

"We've been roaming since morning."

"My cellphone battery died. But it had lasted me about five hours after I got here." He sounded angry. "Of course, there was no network, so the phone was useless anyway. Except for light."

Why didn't he tell her his story? Frustration welled up in her. How could a father abandon his own son? What sort of family deserted their own? How did they imagine he'd return home? She had so many questions, yet Fela ignored it. He didn't seem eager to do anything. She opened her bundle and brought out a bottle of water.

"Go easy on the water."

She took a long gulp till it dripped on her chest. "What does it matter to you? You don't care if I die here or not."

Fela arched an eyebrow. "I'd die before I let you die."

She bolted to her feet. "Who are you? I don't understand any of this. I'm trying to be strong, but I'm afraid."

He locked his gaze with hers. "We are in the middle of nowhere, trying to survive. I'm older and stronger than you. It's my duty to protect you."

"I know nothing about you, besides your name, Fela. And I'm not going to follow you until I know the whole truth."

He shrugged. "Okay. Let's make a deal. I believe we can find a better place to rest and spend the night. When we get there, I'll tell you about me."

"No."

"Be reasonable. We still have a few hours before dark. Why sit here and waste the day?"

His rationale made sense, but she struggled with a decision. He seemed harmless. He had rescued her, given her something to cover her nakedness, fed her. If he'd wanted to kill her, he could have done it sooner.

Fela stood, tied up her bundle, and lifted it. She reluctantly balanced it on her head. From the way he lifted his, she could tell it was heavier than hers. For now she had no option, but she resolved to hear his story in full. Whatever difference it would make.

Chapter Fourteen

Fela found a big tree with heavy branches and decided to rest for the night. It was too dark to see their path any longer. Birds chirped and animal sounds gave him the creeps, but he held his fears together, knowing it could affect Temly.

He pitied her. It was an unfamiliar emotion, not what he experienced at home. But home seemed to be another life. He couldn't find the strength to talk about it. What could he do when she would not follow him any further if he didn't tell her what happened? He wasn't the talking type, except with Law, who understood him. His sisters gave up on getting him to open up long ago.

Temly fell on her knees the moment he helped remove the bundle from her head. She untied it and found her half bottle of water. Within seconds, she'd finished it and opened another. They had only ten left, and Fela wondered how far it would take them.

He let down his load as well, and sat on the ground. She gave him water, and he took a few gulps. They both opened biscuits and munched. Her shoulders slumped with visible exhaustion. Such a child. He brought out their makeshift bed and spread it.

"Lie down."

Temly scrambled onto the bed without argument. He took some water and poured it on her feet. She moaned, confirming his suspicion that her feet were sore. He massaged them gently and then wrapped them in cloth torn from their supplies.

"I think we have to make shoes for you or you won't be able to walk tomorrow."

She moaned a reply he took as "yes." He'd pulled off his shoes for her, but her feet were so much smaller. She'd never be able to walk in them.

He gathered the supplies together and drew them close in hopes animals would not scavenge them, got on the bed with her, and covered them both with the thick red cloth.

"It feels safer under this thick red cloth," Temly whispered.

Fela shrugged. "I thought it would make animals think we are not alive."

"I hope there are no scavengers then."

"Don't think about them."

"Unless they hear us."

He chuckled. "Your imagination is going crazy." He wished he'd been admitted into Boy Scouts or some other para-military group for boys, and then he'd know how to make a fire or something.

"I'm amazed how you can joke in this place."

"I try to laugh off my tragedy."

"They say laughter is the best medicine."

He laughed. "Yeah?" He sighed. "You won't believe I'm a pastor's son. And my dad brought me here."

She sucked in her breath. "To do what?"

"I—it started like—I noticed he had a room, a prayer room he never let anyone go into. I duplicated the key and went inside." He paused for a long time, trying to decide how to tell her this horrid story.

"Why did you—he—why would your dad do so? I mean, not let anyone into his prayer room?"

Fela snickered. "*Oh*, he did a lot. I mean, I'm not—I wasn't close to—Let me start from the beginning." He closed his eyes for only a second.

"I'm the first child of my parents." He paused. "Mom always said I was too inquisitive, and it would get me into trouble. I always had this impression my parents hated me. I never fit into their lives. I hated our church. My sisters did everything my parents wanted, so I ended up being the black sheep. My little brother is still a baby."

"I'm so sorry."

"One day, I opened the prayer room." He closed his eyes and tried not to think. Not to remember how terrified he was of what he saw.

"I entered and immediately I—disappeared."

"Disappeared?"

"I couldn't feel myself. I couldn't see myself. I don't know how to say this, Temly. I sound insane."

"I am in a bad dream myself." Temly's giggle ended in a sob. "I never imagined this kind of life existed."

"I was terrified. I thought of my friend, Law. He was the only one who knew about this. About me. He cut the key for me because he knew I'd try to enter the room when everyone went to church." Fela swallowed. "Then the door opened, and Dad walked in. Since I could see him, I thought he could see me, too."

"What was the room like?"

"Empty. Nothing was in the room."

"I don't understand. What did your dad do?"

"He turned around quickly and ran back out."

"He sensed a strange presence?"

"I guess." Fela squeezed his eyes shut. "I left the room and ran to mine. My heart beat so fast. I'd never been in such pain and fear. Dad came to my room. He knocked and entered. He gave me a once-over and said he was going for a night vigil, did I want to come?"

"What did you say?"

"I told him no. He gave me a small lecture about going to Hell and left." Fela sighed. "He normally gave those annoying little lectures. But I kept thinking, what's my dad up to?"

"He planned to bring you here."

"I don't know. I still don't know. After dinner, I decided to follow him. I got into his Jeep and hid on the floor of the back seat."

"Why didn't you just follow him? He offered."

"I hated to do what he wanted. I loathed him, and the feeling was mutual."

"My dad rules my world. I can't even imagine the word hate used for him. He's everything I think has to do with love."

"*Ain't* you lucky?"

Fela stared at Temly under the thick dark cover. He couldn't see the expression on her face but looking at her gave him some form of inner strength to go on.

"Dad didn't go for a night vigil, he came here."

"*Oh*, no."

Fela swallowed.

"When he got out of the car, I stood slowly and saw him walk over to where you people were tied. He spoke to the thugs. There were many people, but he pointed at the pregnant woman. Then he walked back to the Jeep."

"*Oh* no." Temly sucked in her breath. "Aunty Martha."

"I jumped out of the car. It was a reflex action. I should have just lay there the moment I saw him turn back."

Temly's voice became hoarse. "Did he see you? What did he say?"

"He shouted my name. I was crying so hard. He moved toward me, but I ran from him. He got into his Jeep and drove off." He drew in a ragged breath. "I ran further into the bush so the thugs would not find me. I don't know for how long I ran. I got lost.

"I found this particular tree, retraced my steps, and found the shrine with the food. I went back to the shrine the following night. But yesterday, I lost my way and found you."

"My goodness. I can't—how could he—how—"

"*Shh*." Fela gripped Temly's shoulder. "Do you hear something?"

Chapter Fifteen

Asabi sat with the Coles at dinner where everyone ate spaghetti with beef sauce and mixed vegetables.

She picked at her food while the conversation centered on the search for Temly. The future seemed so bleak; she found it hard to understand what others were saying. This couldn't be a worse nightmare than the abuse she'd already experienced. Where was Temly? Was she being tortured? Was she dead? Did she have—?

Mr. Cole coughed. "You're not eating your food, Asabi."

Asabi raised her head and noticed all eyes were on her. How could she eat when it was her fault Temly was missing? She could have ridden the school bus with Temly and shared her plans.

She shook her head. "I'm not hungry."

Tunji took in a shuddering breath. "None of us feel hungry, Asabi. But we have to eat."

"They found the taxi Temly boarded on her way to school," Mr. Cole said.

He didn't smile, so the news wasn't good. But the only good news Asabi wanted was to hear Temly had been found.

"I know I should be positive. But this is all my fault." Asabi couldn't control her tears.

No one said anything, unlike before when they would fuss over her. She sobbed until she was spent. Temly's family grieved as well and allowing her to stay with them was more than kind, but things had changed. A coldness she didn't understand laced everyone's attitude.

"I will find her or die trying." She jumped to her feet and ran out of the room.

No one came to see her. They probably decided to finish their meals and grieve in silence. Asabi hugged Temly's pillow and mourned the times they'd spent in this room together. She inhaled what was left of her friend's perfume and gasped at the pain brought on by the memory. She thought of their pillow fights or when they cuddled together to gossip and giggle.

When she left her home with Temly's parents, she'd wanted to find comfort with the Coles. It wasn't so. The pain and grief she felt here was too strong. Temly's loving family was no longer the same.

Agony creased Mrs. Cole's face, making her look ten years older. Asabi had thought she was the most beautiful mother on earth, but now she appeared small and shrunken. She'd been encouraged to bath, eat, and rest. A doctor had come in earlier in the evening to prescribe sleeping medication for her. Nothing brought a smile to Mrs. Cole's face. Asabi felt even more miserable than all the times Femi Filips had touched her.

There was a soft knock on the door, and Tunji walked in. Asabi squared her shoulders. There was a time when she'd had such a huge crush on him. His rugged good looks were appealing, and he had a thin moustache he nursed like a baby. His hair was cut short, conditioned, and wavy. Tunji's body was well toned, his muscles developing. What Asabi found most attractive were his dark eyes, taut cheeks, his oblong face, and the way he joked easily. She'd wanted to tell him about her stepfather and have him kill the pedophile for her. This was years ago. Now Tunji was just Temly's big brother and hero. Nothing more.

He sat on the edge of Temly's bed. "It's hard, Asabi. None of us have the words to say how we feel." His voice cracked. "No one ever expected this kind of thing would happen to our family."

Asabi avoided his gaze. He acted so disconcerted, like a little child. Tunji was twenty, but right now he seemed ten years younger, fragile, and weak.

"I'm so sorry." Asabi wished she could turn the hand of time and do everything in a different way.

"This is why I came in here. Stop apologizing. It's not your fault."

"It is." She covered her face. "I should have been on the bus."

"I'm sure you had a good reason."

"I was selfish. My reasons are selfish. I know you all hate me." She couldn't bear any more of the anguish she saw on Tunji's strained face. "Your mom can't bear to look at me. I caused all this."

"If she felt so you wouldn't be in our house right now." Tunji cupped Asabi's face. "She takes solace in the fact you're here. You help her remember the good times with Temly."

She wished she could believe his words, but how? "God knows I would trade my life for hers."

Tunji pulled her into his arms and patted her till her sobs quieted.

"The governor has launched a major campaign to find Temly." Tunji licked his lips. "We need you to be strong."

It was the least she could do. "I will do anything to help." She nodded. "I'm strong. I am strong."

"Uncle is throwing his executive weight on this. He has gone on national television and called on people who have information to come forward."

Asabi sat forward. "What should I do?"

Tunji shrugged. "Nothing for now. But people are coming forward with tales of their friends and family gone missing." Tunji shut his eyes tight for just a flash in time. "It seems there's a terrible siege going on right now. A kidnapping spree."

Long after Tunji left, Asabi sat in the darkness. If it was a siege, as Tunji said, then there may be people with information. It gave her hope that Temly was not alone. It was like being in school, and the whole class was punished.

Asabi switched on the television in Temly's room and tuned in to national news. She needed to find the other people with Temly's kind of story. She no longer felt welcome here. Temly's family didn't act as awesome as she'd known them to be. No one smiled or said nice things to one another. Least of all to her.

Chapter Sixteen

Lawrence the barber had nothing much going for him besides his shop. When Fela nudged him about thinking of a woman, he'd been right, as the boy usually was. But Fela would never believe the kind of woman in Law's life at the moment, and for the first time since taking the boy under his wing, he didn't have the mind to tell the truth. Things were complicated.

He opened the steel door to his accommodations and took a moment to accustom his eyes to the dark, a habit he'd formed since the first day he moved here. He'd had one too many experiences of things jumping out of the darkness. If anything, or anyone were hiding in his space, he'd rather kill it in the dark.

In his previous life, when he was into relationships, he feared nothing. Now his heart thudded. He had gone on a wild goose chase, spent all he had. And what a fool he'd made of himself. Fela would have had a fit, laughing. The boy was the only thing he had now, along with his barbing salon, which only shifted him slightly away from the category of the begging populace.

He flipped on the switch expecting to see him, Fela, his boy, sprawled on the mat on the floor, but the room was empty. As familiar as he was with this place, it showed how hollow his life was. He kicked one of the two barber chairs out of his way. He'd been away for just four days, and everything remained as he'd left it. He thought Fela would have come and moved the air around, stay. He'd know. Why hadn't his boy called? Though he was glad he hadn't.

He hadn't been kidding about Fela's ability to see into the future or tell of the past. Despite being the son of a renowned preacher and deciding instead to pitch his tent with a barber who had no respect for religion, his gift and calling remained. Pastor Favor had told Law that his son would take over the church one day. Suffice to say, the two men had no love lost.

Law opened his small refrigerator and removed the bread he bought on Sunday night. The same number of slices he left was there, and he lost appetite just looking at it. There was a can of Red Bull, and he took it instead.

He slid to the floor and gulped the drink. What next? The cool drink soothed his parched throat. He couldn't remember the last time he had anything to eat or drink. The rat race his life had become was tiring. He wanted more. Or less.

Ten years earlier, he'd thought about ending it all. He was alone just like now, and all was lost. He didn't have even the shop at the time. Then he'd walked into Favor Peter's church and met Fela, and the boy had sparked something in him. A most unlikely friendship with a boy he thought could be his.

He'd picked up his wits and gone to look for a job as a barber, and through the years climbed back up till he got this place. Over the years, Fela had torn himself from his family and connected with him.

But Law was back in the dreary alley again. One click, and everything he thought he left far behind faced him. A useless existence, and an emptiness no one seemed able to fill. Not even Fela anymore.

He finished his drink. Maybe he should leave Warri. He could sell his salon and start over. Too many happenings in the last year. The buildup had climaxed, and he was left with nothing. Just like ten years ago.

Or he could take the plunge he'd fought before. Take poison and end it all. Fela may find him after a few days. Much as he loved the boy, he had been unstable over the years. Sometimes he would spend days holed up in the salon, and then he'd disappear for weeks. He sometimes called, and sometimes did not. Law had had enough.

He rolled over onto the mat and pulled out his pillow from under the worktable. He'd won the urge to commit suicide after a friend invited him to church. But not now. Church didn't work, and he was back to square one.

No one needed to tell him what to do. Voices he'd once battled argued in his head, and one spoke to the coward in him.

"Lawrence, the barber, it's time to face your demon. Death."

His head shot up but there was nobody in the room with him.

Chapter Seventeen

The Delta sun had risen early and was high before noon, promising a scorching day.

Asabi checked the piece of paper in her hand again, just to be sure as she walked from the bus station where she had been dropped off. She felt safe meeting this woman, since she was a pastor's wife. She felt comfortable here. She hoped to work with her. Her son had disappeared just as abruptly as Temly. The stories mimicked each other too much for Asabi to ignore.

The streets had filled despite the heat. Asabi was usually in school during this time, though it was Saturday, and she was amazed at the number of people out on the road. This city couldn't be much busier than Ibadan, could it?

She stopped a taxi with a level of trepidation and mentioned the street she was going to. The taxi driver nodded. Perhaps her heavy make-up made her look older and the driver thought she was rich because the fare seemed high to her, but after several moments of haggling over the price, she got in. And if she disappeared like Temly, well, she deserved it.

Refinery Road was not far enough for the fare charged, but Asabi was grateful she got to her destination. She paid the fare and heaved her small luggage out of the taxi.

Mrs. Precious Peter hadn't arrived at the church yet, and Asabi was asked to wait in the main hall. She didn't mind. She hated how she had to leave Temly's house without any information but felt this was what she needed to do. To look for Temly anywhere she could. Any means she could. After spending yesterday afternoon and evening with Temly's family, she couldn't stay. She'd rather die than stay when their sorrow was her fault.

Asabi had never entered such a church before. The hall bespoke affluence. Not like the more traditional ones she endured with her parents or Temly's, where everything was glum, and she was constantly reminded she needed to repent of her many sins. This church breathed life.

The altar was decorated with gold, blue silk, and satin, with marble floors and walls. Flowerpots and potted plants graced every aisle. The seats, over a thousand of them if Asabi could count, were cushioned with deep blue velvet. The large hall was air-conditioned, and for a moment, Asabi wanted to forget her troubles and her reason for being here. Exhaustion threatened her, but she couldn't rest until Temly was found.

Many thoughts ran through her mind. Temly's family would be upset to find her gone, but her disappearance would make sense when—if—she found and brought Temly back to them.

She had never been courageous in her life. Ten years of sexual abuse had done nothing but make her vulnerable. Until now.

"Ms. Asabi Ajayi."

Asabi jolted and saw a lady by a door close to the altar. "Yes, ma'am."

"Mama Peter will see you now."

Asabi stood. "Thank you, ma'am."

Her palms sweated despite the cool air. She'd never taken any initiative before now, not without Temly. Yet she was here. Excitement crept into her blood, causing a tsunami. No matter what happened, she'd never regret coming here.

Mrs. Peter, or Mama Peter as the lady preferred, had more wrinkles and folds than she did on screen. Asabi thought she was much larger, too. She wore heavy make-up and gold rings on both hands but no other jewelry. Her hair was swept up in a high bun. She wasn't pretty, but her fair complexion made her attractive. The lady pointed her to one of several velvety seats in the office and took another.

The room was so cold Asabi shuddered. "Thank you for seeing me, ma'am."

"You're welcome, my dear. Hope it wasn't difficult for you to find the church."

"No, ma'am."

The lady Asabi assumed was a secretary took a picture of Asabi before she could stop her.

Asabi covered her face. "No, please. No pictures."

Mama Peter's jaw dropped, and the secretary gasped.

"Why? Are you a secret agent?"

What sort of a question was that? "No. But I am a teenager. My mom must not see me on TV. I'm only here to help to find my friend."

Mama Peter nodded at the secretary. "Don't take any more pictures."

Asabi sighed. "Thank you, ma'am."

"Now, tell me all about yourself. And what do you need from me."

"You said your son went missing at about the same time my friend disappeared. I want to join forces with you to find my friend," Asabi said.

"Why? Don't you have a family?"

"I do, but they don't care. My friend's family is too confused. I want to join your family."

"You believe it's the same kidnappers?"

"I'm willing to find out. Please, ma'am. I came all the way from Ibadan to find my friend. When I saw you on TV last night, I knew we could work together." Asabi swallowed. She refused to be sent away now. She had nowhere to go.

With her savings over the years, she had enough money to sustain herself, but for how long? She couldn't begin looking for another family and couldn't go back to Ibadan.

What if she could?

"What did you say is your first name again?"

"Asabi."

"And what is the name of your missing friend?"

"Temilola Cole. We all call her Temly."

Mama Peter frowned. "Temilola Cole."

The secretary's face lit up. "She's the Oyo State governor's niece. Governor Tai Cole. She's the one the governor launched the campaign about."

Mama Peter's face expanded into a wide smile, and the layers of thick foundation on her face seemed to develop cracks. "*Ah*, the governor's *daughter* is your friend? Why didn't you say so?"

Asabi wondered why Mama Peter hadn't yet mentioned her son. She cringed at the enthusiasm displayed about being a friend of the governor's niece and no mention of her being underage, staying away from her family, or wearing bold eyebrows and red lipstick. Still, this was just a beginning. She was here now, and she planned to see it through.

Chapter Eighteen

Temly shook Fela awake.

He sat up drowsily. "Is it morning yet?"

"I guess. I'm not well. What happened last night?"

He stretched and yawned. "Who knows?" He stood. "Stay here."

Temly threw the red cover off. She glanced at the makeshift garment; she'd stained it again. This was so hard. Did Fela notice? She hoped not.

"I won't stay here alone."

"I'm just going to look around." He walked a little distance while she followed him with her eyes. "You can clean up. I see footprints. Animal footprints."

He knew, *huh*! She was mortified at the mere thought and convinced herself otherwise. She took his advice, rinsed off the stain as much as she could, changed her little piece of makeshift cloth-pad, and rolled up the bed. She analyzed the supplies and wondered how long a few packets of biscuits, sweets, and water would last.

"The biscuits won't last more than three or four days. And the water maybe seven if we ration it."

Fela walked back to her. "Give no thought for tomorrow, for sufficient to the day is the evil."

She pressed her lips together in consternation. "What does it mean?"

"It's Scripture."

"I thought you were the black sheep of the family. And you didn't read your Bible."

He pinched his imaginary beard. "I grew up in church. These things just stick in your head." He rolled his bundle. "What we heard last night might have been a herd of cows or something. I saw hoof prints."

"What does it mean?"

"If they were a herd of cows?" He shrugged. "It may be safe to follow them. Maybe not."

"What do we do?"

"I don't know the hooves of animals so well. I grew up in the city."

Temly sat. Better to retain her little energy and grab some breakfast. She opened a packet of biscuits and handed it to Fela. He eased down beside her, and she opened another for herself.

"Ibadan?"

"No, Warri."

"Your dad drove here from Warri?" Temly's jaw dropped. "Delta state?"

"Yes. Are you from Ibadan?"

The truth drove Temly to near hysterics. Ibadan was at least two hundred and fifty miles from Warri. If Fela's dad drove to this forest from Warri and her captors drove from Ibadan, where could this be?

"Yes," she whispered. "We could be anywhere." Familiar shudders of fear ran through her. "We could be anywhere."

"See it like this," Fela said, though Temly read doubt and fear in his eyes. "We could be anywhere between the two cities. I know Warri like the back of my hand. And you know Ibadan, right?"

Temly nodded. Not well, she thought, but it wasn't important now. She could communicate in Ibadan, could find her way home, or at least to the State House.

"So, we have an advantage. We can get to two cities. And I know Onitsha, which is close to Warri. You probably know Lagos, as well."

"A little."

Fela munched on his biscuit. Temly ate, too, confused and so weary. Maybe they should have stayed close to the shrine and pray one day it would be discovered and raided. And they'd be found, instead of running into this wild place. Left to Fela, he would live the rest of his life eating food sacrificed to some god.

Temly stared at him. He was lost in thought. Maybe he now had regrets, too.

"You think we should find our way back to the shrine?"

Fela jolted. "What?"

"Should we find our way back to the shrine? One day, someone will discover the shrine and it will be raided and we will be rescued. What's the use of staying here and starving?"

He chuckled. "You've been watching too many cartoons."

Temly burst into tears. "You think this is funny?"

Fela scooted toward her and rubbed her back. "I'm sorry. It's okay."

She pushed off his hand. Insensitive pig. Lost in the middle of two cities in the forest, and he thought she watched too many cartoons?

He glanced behind them. "I was thinking of the hooves, footprints. Not knowing what kind of animal. Not knowing if they'd lead us to water or to people who could help us. This is not funny, and I'm not making fun of you."

Temly sniffed. Was there a better word than tired for how she felt? Exhausted came close. She wished Fela's words carried some comfort, but they didn't. She touched the red sand on the ground and came away with some. Tiny stones in the mix brought her to reality.

"Though I may not love and serve God like my parents and their congregation, I put my trust in Him. I know He exists, somewhere. And if I am still alive today, there is hope for us."

Temly stared at him through her tears. His words made sense. There had to be a reason for this horrible ordeal.

He narrowed his eyes. "On my thirteenth birthday, I decided to start growing my hair."

Temly's eyes were drawn to his cornrows, now rough and tangled at the edges. Why was he telling her this? To take her mind off the nightmare?

"One of my parents, I don't know which, would wait until I slept then cut part of it. I'd wake up and resist, and the cut would look horrible. Still, I refused to visit the barbershop."

"To offend them? You must have proved nasty, I'm sure."

He nodded. "One day, I woke up tied like Samson. My hair was all gone."

Chapter Nineteen

Asabi arrived at the Peters' home in one of two vehicles.

Pastor Favor Peter came in with his daughters, fourteen-year-old Gold and ten-year-old Diamond, while Mama Peter arrived a few minutes later with their son, two-year-old Olive, Asabi, and two house-servants, Davida and Mabel.

The house was palatial, and bright security lights gleamed on shiny marble stones. With white leather furniture in the lobby, the formal room depicted immense wealth. Family pictures graced the walls along with beautiful artwork. Asabi gasped at the sight of gold and silver crockery lined on a mantle place.

She had little to learn from this family about respect. The Peter girls rushed to their mother when she stepped through the door with Asabi without so much as a "*welcome, Mom,*" and took her handbag.

Amidst laughter and scowling, Mama Peter tried to take her bag from her daughters' searching hands. They took money, snacks, and got into a fight as the greedy Gold tried to use her position as the eldest to cheat her sister.

Asabi found fault with her own mother on many issues, but at least Eni had taught her manners. Not Gold and Diamond. They continued to bicker and scream until their father joined everyone for dinner, and then she saw a different side of the girls. They sat quietly and ate. The reverent attitude in their father's presence made her sneer.

After dinner, Papa Peter, as Asabi discovered he was called even at home, sat with the family in a living room more like the lobby of a five-star hotel and recounted his grief of losing his son. Fela had been gone for almost a week, and the pastor found it hard to even trust God.

Everyone listened with rapt attention. Asabi watched their every move, the way they respected their father, who behaved like he had some strange powers to hypnotize anyone.

She couldn't help but compare this household with hers and Temly's—before the tragedy. So different. What was a family supposed to be like?

Papa Peter seemed to stare through people. Something about the hollowness in his eyes made him seem—amoral. Asabi hated the creepy feeling his see-through gaze dispatched. He didn't turn like other people but moved his body like he had a stiff neck. Nothing about him seemed right to her.

She studied his profile, his hard mouth and flaring nose. He narrowed his eyes a lot, which made his wide, muscular face appear menacing. Asabi didn't like him much, among other reasons, because he was so thickset, tall, and dark. And scary. He ignored her like she was a stray dog.

Mama Peter seemed to worship the ground her husband walked on. Asabi watched her kneel to serve him a glass of water and speak softly to him. Several times, she stood to wipe imaginary sweat off his face. Her smile at him seemed fake, but it came often. Okay, Asabi hadn't been to church except for a few occasions with Temly, and she'd never known the type of worship these Christians engaged in, but this seemed—strange.

After the chat with Mama Peter, Asabi had been made to attend an evening prayer meeting where Fela, the missing first child of the Peters, had been prayed for with worshippers screaming at the top of their voices, sweating in the air-conditioned room, and speaking a—language.

Papa Peter now spoke the language again, and Asabi closed her eyes. She wished she could learn more about these odd people.

Mama Peter had welcomed her into their home only because Temly was the Governor's niece, but could she have made a mistake with her choice to come here? She'd hoped they would be her new family until Temly was found. If Temly was found. Now she had her doubts about staying.

When she'd watched the news the previous night and seen several people interviewed, she had chosen the Peters because she felt a connection with them. Had she made a blunder she would regret?

Gold and Diamond moved to kneel in front of their father. In the most bizarre manner, he laid hands on their heads and blessed them. One by one, other members of the household, Olive, Mama Peter, Davida, and Mabel, all went to kneel before the man.

"Asabi, you, too." Mama Peter nudged her. "Though you are not saved, God has chosen to have mercy on you. Go and take the blessing."

Asabi knelt in front of the man of God and waited. He spoke the strange language over her head and then laid ice-cold hands on her forehead.

"You are a troubled child," he said. "You need salvation. And you will be saved before you leave."

Asabi raised her head. "Amen." She swallowed hard.

What salvation did he mean? Could Papa Peter know of her predicament at home by some divine revelation? She shuddered. She didn't feel comfortable to have a stranger know her innermost secrets, but back in school, she'd heard of prophets who could read people's minds and future.

He waved her away, and she crawled back to her position beside the house servants. Mabel opened the front door and people trooped in to receive a blessing.

A man tripped in front of Asabi after taking the blessing and fell to his knees before her. She shrank.

The man whispered, "Outside the gate, come. Please."

She gazed into a pair of dark eyes. He was dressed in plain green T-shirt and black trousers and wore his hair in dreadlocks neatly tied at his nape. The person behind the man helped him up. He nodded in appreciation, caught her attention again, and walked out of the room.

Asabi's heart thudded. What did the request mean? Outside the gate? Who was he? How did he know her?

About an hour later, the parade of those seeking blessings came to an end, and Asabi was taken to a fancy en suite guest room with a king-size bed where she laid her weary body on cool, clean, white sheets. She needed to return a buzz from Tunji. He had called and sent several text messages, demanding her whereabouts. It was only fair to keep him updated.

She composed a simple text message, apologizing for her sudden disappearance, assuring him she was now safe and, on a mission, to find Temly. Her luxurious bedroom was all white with floor tiles, and floor-to-ceiling lace curtains. Where was Temly? She sank her head into two soft pillows and thought of her friend. Did she have a bed to lie on and food?

Asabi leaned forward and checked her image in a full-length mirror mounted on the wall by the door. Her make-up was gone, and the weariness of the day made her look her age, perhaps younger. She smoothed her sweaty hand over the soft fabric of her skirt and steeled her resolve. The strange man came to mind.

She found her way to the front door, eased it open, and walked to the gate, hoping no one would see her. The security man at the gate mistook her for one of the visitors and let her out.

Outside, Asabi followed the direction where shops lined the street. She didn't know what to expect or why she bothered to come at all. Mid-way, a man called to her from the other side of the road, a dual carriageway. She recognized his voice from earlier.

"I just about gave up."

If Temly had been kidnapped, Asabi didn't want the same experience. She stole a glance at the man. He walked at her pace. The shops along the street were all closed, the road deserted. The night air was cool, and she shivered.

"Who are you?" she said.

"My name is Lawrence."

"What do you want?"

"To talk about Fela."

"I don't know him."

"But you came because of him." He paused. "I've had my eyes on the family. I got information when you arrived."

Asabi stopped walking. He stopped as well. "I came because—I can't talk to you. I don't know you. Please go away."

"I want to find Fela. I have reason to believe he's alive."

"I don't know how to help you."

"But you came here from Ibadan. You came to find Fela, too."

"No, I didn't." This was crazy, being here out in the open and risking her life. She spun round and changed direction back to where she came from. "You got your information wrong. Please, leave me alone."

"You have gone to the wrong people. Fela's parents don't care about him."

Asabi froze when he touched her arm. She hadn't noticed when he crossed the road to her. She hated human touch, and more so by men.

"We need to talk." Lawrence lowered his voice. "Ask the gateman to show you Law's shop. I'm there day and night."

He was gone just as quietly as he'd come.

Goosebumps covered Asabi's arms, and she clasped her hand over her mouth. Her heartbeat against her chest so hard she feared it would explode. She ran to the gate and the gateman opened it with a frown. Not ready to heed the security man's demand, she rushed to the front door and stepped inside.

A firm hand grabbed her, and she came face to face with the dead eyes of Papa Peter.

"Where do you think you are going?"

Chapter Twenty

Papa Peter's face came close to Asabi's, and she attempted to free herself from his grip.

"Please, sir, I wanted to buy airtime for my phone."

He gawked. "You lie. My spirit tells me you are a liar."

She slid out of his hold. "No, sir."

"You say your missing friend is the daughter of the governor of Oyo state."

"The niece, sir."

"Why are you so bent on finding her? Are your parents aware you are here?"

"Yes." What could she say? "My friend and I are like twins, and her parents know I am here, too."

Papa Peter squinted. "I am a man of God. I see through the soul. You ran away from home and now you are here. You are evil. You seduce men. You will go to Hell."

Asabi stepped back. "I want to find my friend." A sob escaped her lips. "I just want to find my friend. Please help me, sir. If you are a man of God, and you know the truth, tell me where Temly is."

"She's in an evil forest."

"Where?" Asabi screamed. "Where?"

Mama Peter walked into the parlor in her housecoat. A frown creased her forehead. "What are you doing here? Aren't you in bed?"

"I had to buy airtime—"

Papa Peter pointed toward the guest room. "Go inside!"

Asabi hurried away and only felt better with the door shut. She pressed a hand to her chest, thankful the woman had come to rescue her. She closed her eyes and allowed her pounding heartbeat to return to normal.

A loud cracking sound made her heart leap back into a fast beat. Mama Peter's harsh words followed the sound.

"Tell me what you were doing with her!"

Asabi pressed her face against the white panel door. Another sharp sound. A slap on the face? Mama Peter slapped the man of God? It seemed impossible. Or was it the other way? Did this man of God hit his wife? What else would she experience in this house? She wished she could see what was happening.

"Tell me, you liar!"

"I did not touch her. Ask her."

"I warn you. If I find out you touched her—"

"I did not."

"I will ask her to leave in the morning."

Papa Peter raised his voice. "You don't have to. She's harmless."

His wife's voice matched his. "You want her around, don't you?"

"No. I never touch any of them, believe me."

Asabi heard fast footfalls and closed her eyes. Was Papa Peter abusive like Femi Filips, too? Why did this kind of men exist at all? She sat on the bed and waited for any more drama. Weary, she ran her palms over the cool sheets. The bed beckoned, and she laid her head on the soft pillow.

Mixed emotions prevented her from sleeping. The question kept coming back to her. Had she made the right choice to come? Maybe she should leave on her own in the morning. How could the woman slap her "man of God" husband? What kind of relationship did they have? In all her years of seeing her mother married to Femi Filips, he'd never raised his hand on her or vice versa.

Lawrence crept into her thoughts. He said the family wasn't interested in finding their son, but how could this be true? Who was Law? Why would he want to talk to her? Why did he think she came because of someone she didn't know? Who was his informant? So many questions and no answers.

She would have loved to follow up on Law, but she couldn't risk the unknown. The old, terrified Asabi came back and she shivered at the thought of being here with a man who might be like her stepfather.

She opened her bag and brought out her notebook. There were four families interviewed the previous night. The other three families were in Ibadan. All three families had grown-up sons missing. One of the missing was a married man. Maybe it would be wise to go back home. In the comfort of Temly's house, she could better join forces to find her friend instead of risking her life to stay with strange people.

No matter what this family portrayed in public, they were weird, and she feared what could happen if she stayed with them. It would be best to return home.

Another strange thought occurred to her. She could follow her initial plan and search for her biological father. She had an address and money. When she was settled, she could return to find out about Temly. As it was, she could do nothing here for Temly except wait and pray her friend was found.

But what if she chose to stay? They had a lot of money. The church was large, and the pastor lived like a king. Could she be normal in the morning and see what they would do? See if Mama Peter asked her to leave?

There was a knock on her door, and she jolted. For a moment, she closed her eyes and feigned sleep. Should she respond? The thrashing of her blood in her veins became louder than the horn of a truck, deafening her ears. She sank deeper into the soft folds of the bed, willing to disappear.

"Asabi?"

Papa Peter sounded strange. What did he want? Had he come back after his wife left, just to assault her? Did she come here only to be raped by a strange man? *O God, please help me.*

"I'm going for a night vigil. Do you want to come along?"

Chapter Twenty-One

Fela chose to follow the hoof prints.

Temly didn't want to argue with him, but deep inside, she fought with the decision. The sun rose, and they hiked through the forest until they broke into less dense grassland. Egrets flew high in the sky.

Fela shielded his eyes. "Those birds show there is a sign of life ahead somewhere."

Temly grunted a response. When she was much younger, she would sing the birdsong. Not now.

"You remember the song about painting the fingers white?" Fela sang. "*Leke-leke*, give me a white finger. *Leke-leke*, give me a white finger."

Temly rolled her eyes, and Fela shut his mouth. She knew she must seem odd to him. One minute she was like a child and in the next, she'd fight a lion. She didn't understand herself these days either.

They walked uphill, and Temly found it hard to breathe. It didn't help much when the heavens opened, and rain poured on them in its *Deltan* fury. Unable to find cover, they continued till the blinding rain hindered further movement.

Fela found a lone tree in the hilly landscape, and Temly followed. They pressed their wet bodies against the trunk of the tree until the rain subsided.

"Seems we are going uphill, Temly."

She nodded. She thought of the meager supplies in their bundles and how her teeth chattered without control. She bit her lower lip to keep from crying out.

"Are you alright?"

Temly gaged him through hot tears. "We'll freeze to death."

"No, we won't." Fela held her gaze. "I'll look away. You'll take your clothes off, pass to me, and I will squeeze with all my strength, then you can put it on again."

Temly sniffed. "What will it do?"

"I don't know. But we can try." He hesitated. "Your—period. Are you—is it—?"

Temly shrugged, too embarrassed to answer. She'd tried not to think about it. So far, she was wet all over. All their clothes, including the bedding was drenched. Even if they got dry, which was unlikely, the bedding would not. If it had rained in the morning, and then became sunny now, there would have been hope—

"Take no thought for the morrow. For which one of you can add to his life by taking thought."

"Another scripture?"

Fela pulled off his jeans. "Yes. They keep dancing in my head."

"What are you doing?"

"I don't know what this can do for me now." He dropped his jeans on the ground and pulled off his T-shirt. "I'll squeeze my clothes first, and you can wear them while I squeeze yours."

She murmured. "A hero."

Fela finished. "I pray we get some sunshine before night."

"No scriptures for back up?" She hated to be sarcastic. He wasn't to blame for their predicament. "I'm sorry."

"You don't need to apologize." He opened his bundle and brought out two cans of malt drink. "Here."

She took one. "Thank you."

"Concerning the works of my hands, command ye me."

Temly couldn't help but smile. "It doesn't make sense to me, sorry."

"I had a friend back at home. Much older than me. Law." He chuckled. "If I am a black sheep, Law is the devil."

"I'm sure your parents didn't approve."

"Approve is a mild word. Law is a barber. He makes my hair for me."

Temly involuntarily glared at his cornrows, wet and dripping.

"Law taught me how to lock my room when I sleep at night after I woke up one morning and all my hair was gone, and I was tied to my bed till evening as my punishment. When Law heard, he was livid. He had a carpenter fix a bolt for me when my folks were in church." Fela shook his head. "I enjoyed saying my scriptures to him, too. He would laugh. Call me confused." He squinted. "I never thought I'd need them till now."

"How old were you then?"

"First lock was three years ago. I was thirteen."

Temly assessed him. His muscles made him look older. Perhaps Law took him to the gym, too.

"And what did your parents do?"

He smirked. "What do you think?"

Temly shrugged. "Pick it?"

"They stopped after the fifth lock. I had a workman put a big latch behind."

He laughed when Temly's eyes widened. "Yeah. Let's see if we can gain some time." He put the soaked bundle on her head and heaved his up as well.

Hours later, it wasn't dark enough to stop the uphill trek, but Temly dropped to the ground. The weather had not improved, and their wet clothing was still plastered to their bodies.

Temly untied her bundle and brought out a half bottle of water and drank it. "Hey!" she called out to Fela, who was unaware she had stopped. Whether he liked it or not, she wasn't going anywhere.

With her eyes closed, she didn't care if he returned or not, though she knew he would. It took several moments before he nudged her with the tip of his shoe.

"Go on, if you want," she murmured.

His bundle hit the ground beside her.

"Back at home, when Mom was so tired she couldn't move her legs, she'd lie down flat like this. I'd have her soak her feet in warm water and then I'd massage them," Temly said.

Fela moved to sit close to her feet and unwrapped the cloth-shoes he'd made for her. She flinched.

"It must hurt badly," he said softly.

Temly shrugged. She thought she was beyond pain until he tried to massage one of her feet. "They look cooked."

Fela knit his eyebrows. "And you accuse me of cracking jokes in this dreary place." He shifted to his bundle and untied it. He removed a bottle of water and brought it to her feet.

"What are you doing?"

"We don't have warm water, but we can use this." He opened the bottle. "Then we can trek an hour or more before we lose all light."

"Two things, Mr. Trekker. I'm not going any further tonight. And you have to plan where we're going, or I won't continue. Second, we don't have the luxury of pouring water on my feet."

"And listen Mrs. Trekker—"

"I'm not your Mrs."

He poured the water. "Whatever."

She moaned, "*Oh*! Feels so good."

Fela laughed. "Can I ask you a question? Where are we?"

"How should I know?"

The forest was not as thick as before, but they could be anywhere in Nigeria or outside the country's boundaries. The evening air grew cooler. Temly couldn't comprehend beyond the numbing cold.

"Exactly. How is anyone to know? We keep moving till we—"

Fela went still.

"Till we? What?"

He gritted his teeth, and Temly saw his eyes bulge. "Don't move. Don't scream."

Temly's heart plunged, and her lips trembled so hard she couldn't stop the clattering sound. Humans, animals? What, *oh* no.

She kept her gaze on Fela, her new navigator. Her neck felt so stiff it might break if she dared shift.

Fela's eyes fluttered close, and he let out a soft sigh. "Turn a little to your left. It's almost all gone."

Temly prepared for anything but the fat, black and gold reptile slithering away. She leapt on Fela, and he caught her in his arms just in time.

She screamed.

Chapter Twenty-Two

Temly clung to Fela's neck and wept like a child.

He squeezed her back and spoke words of comfort to calm her fears. He'd frozen when the big snake slithered along, and crippling fear had gripped him. There was no way he could have hidden it from Temly.

"It's okay, it's all right, baby." He pressed her head to his chest. "It's gone. You'll be fine."

Temly shook her head. "I want to die. I'm so scared, Fela. I want to die."

"You won't die. We'll survive. Even though we walk through the valley of the shadow of death, Temly, God is with us. His rod and staff, they comfort us."

"If you are God, take us out of here. Take us away from here!" Temly screamed.

"He will. He will."

Fela wished God would save them, and he needed Temly to be strong. He held her until her sobs stopped, but when he tried to detach himself, she clung harder. So, he held on. He found some warmth from her body, and it gave him hope.

In his heart, he prayed to a God he'd despised and shunned. *Please get us out of here, Lord. Prove You exist to me. Prove You love my parents and sisters, and all those faithful people who call on You day and night. Give me a sign.*

He laid Temly on the cool grass, but she screeched. "We can't stay here. There may be more snakes. I hate snakes."

"We can move further uphill. Can you walk?"

She slumped and cried more. "No. I can't, I'm tired. I'm tired."

He didn't think she could cry any more, but her shoulders continued to shake. He needed to get away, think. And pray.

As a child, he despised morning and evening devotion. After he started locking his room, he stopped attending altogether. Now he needed God's intervention. Yet he couldn't cry to God the way he wanted. He couldn't weep with Temly broken like this. He was the only hope she had. *If your strength fails in the day of adversity, then your strength is small.*

He closed his eyes, unable to look at Temly's crumbled form. "I need strength, dear Lord. Give me strength like Samson."

Temly shrieked at some ants on the ground and caught his attention. Maybe someone would hear her and come to the rescue. Fela only wanted her to be strong.

"Here." He held out his hand to her. She clung to it, whimpering while he packed the rest of their supplies with his other hand. "You know what, Temly? Carry the supplies, and I'll carry you."

She whimpered and accepted the heavy bundles. Fela lifted her much the same way he'd carried her the first time.

"All the way to Calvary he went for me. He went for me. He went for me. All the way to Calvary he went for me, he died to give me life."

Fela sang the song over and over. His feet weighed a ton; the burden became increasingly too heavy to carry.

"His cross must have weighed more than this," he said. "I mean, the cross Jesus carried to Calvary must have weighed more than this."

"More than what?"

"You. And the bundle."

"I don't know."

He controlled the trembling of his lips with a tight smile. Tears threatened to stream down his face. He couldn't remember the last time he cried, but he had to restrain himself for her sake.

"I know I sinned against God." He sighed. "You never served God with your family, did you?" Temly did not reply. "Are you asleep?"

She was. She became a dead weight in his arms, and he had to put her down. She jumped when her back touched the ground.

"No, don't leave me."

"I'm not leaving. You fell asleep, and the bundle was falling."

"I'm awake now. Let's go."

"I'm tired, Temly." He stretched his neck. "We need to rest."

"I'm afraid. There are snakes here."

"Take your mind off it."

He opened the bundle and prepared a bed. The moon was rising, and the night air was still. He placed the bundle aside and lay flat on his back. Temly crawled over and laid on him. He didn't mind, though he'd never touched a girl before. What she must be going through at such a time as this.

"Lay on the ground, Temly. You can't sleep like this."

She didn't respond, and he got impatient. He shoved her aside and gulped in air. "Don't make this more difficult."

Temly landed on the ground with a small thump and cried. She scrambled away from him and rolled into a ball. He ignored her till he heard her soft sobs. This was so unlike him. He never pitied a crying girl. His sisters, Gold and Diamond, manipulated their Mom all the time with their tears. But this was different.

He pulled her to him and allowed her to half-lay on his chest, and then he wrapped his arms around her and closed his eyes.

Sufficient to the day was the evil thereof.

Chapter Twenty-Three

He knocked on the door, the sound soft and subtle. Five-year-old Asabi sat up and clutched in her arms her precious new teddy bear, Magnum, which she named after her favorite ice-cream stick. He'd bought it for her just today. It was a life-size teddy, same as her height and so fluffy she buried her body in it.

The door shifted and her new daddy popped his head in first before he opened it. His face lit up. But no matter what he did, she thought he was creepy. Mommy just married him a few days ago and she moved into his huge house. He'd bought more toys than anyone ever did for her, and Mommy seemed so happy to be his wife.

Still, she didn't like him. He watched her funny. As small as she was, she knew it was not a good look. He touched her funny, too, when he carried her, which he always liked to do. She wanted to tell him she was no longer a baby and could walk, but Mommy may think she was rude.

He stepped inside, and he had on only his robe tied loosely at the waist.

"Did you call?"

Asabi didn't like to talk to him. She shook her head, and her long, dark locks swung from side to side.

He sat beside her, so close he almost squeezed Magnum. He smoothed back her hair. "You need a new hairstyle."

She wondered why he would bother. Mommy took care of her hair. It was long, thick, and soft, and even the hairdresser liked to make it.

"Mommy said it is beautiful."

The tilt of his lips in an apparition of a smile did not reach his dark eyes. "What does Mommy know about beautiful girls?"

She didn't answer him but she wished her mother would come right in and take him away.

He leaned closer and rubbed her head, drawing her into his arms. "I will take care of you, my sweet darling."

She stiffened in his arms as he continued to move his large hands over her hair and her back.

He pulled her head back, and the face of Papa Peter lowered to hers.

****

Asabi startled awake and gripped the edge of the bed. The room was dark, and there seemed to be someone inside. The hairs on the back of her neck tingled, and she feared to open her eyes. Electricity must have gone out sometime in the night, as the air-conditioning wasn't cool anymore. The same fear she'd experienced the night before came all over her again. Why had she seen the pastor in her childhood room?

She heard a low hiss of the generator moments before her room was flooded with light, and she stifled a scream. The air-conditioner came back on. She opened her eyes, and though she didn't know what to expect, she was surprised to be the only one in the room. She let out a heavy sigh of relief.

She'd had different horrible dreams growing up about Femi Filips, but this one with Papa Peter seemed so weird. She checked her phone for the time; it was too early to wake up.

Why had Papa Peter invited her to a night vigil? Did the whole family attend as well? She couldn't be bothered. She hated the dream, as much as what her life had been in the last ten years after her mother married Femi Filips, after dating for just two months. Many had thought the marriage would not last more than a couple of years. But from the first year, from the first time Femi violated her, he'd told her he would stay married to her mother to be close to her. And once she was of age, marry her.

When her pumping heartbeat slowed, Asabi sandwiched her head between two pillows and planned her next move. She had to consider Law, the Peters, the Coles, her father. What would she do next to chart the course of her life?

She had told her father she would meet him in Lagos but had not. She'd thought he would send her a message, but he didn't. Maybe he hadn't been there at all. Maybe he wasn't real. He rarely posted anything on social media and had restricted his social life online to only one. Besides a few messages he exchanged with her mother, he never said anything on his wall. And he had been slow in responding to her messages and her anxiety to meet. She couldn't follow that route anymore. Maybe someday, when Temly was found, she could pick it up again.

There was the Peters. What could they do for her? Seeing Papa Peter in her nightmare, and after he knocked on her door, after Mama Peter challenged him about her, was it even remotely safe to stay?

And Law. She was intrigued. How did he know her and why she came? She'd been timid most of her life, but sometimes her cat-curiosity popped up. Just like now. Should she take his invitation and find his shop? What would she discover if she followed his route? He seemed only interested in finding Fela. How would this help her search for Temly?

And finally, there was her most sensible option. To go back to the Coles and beg their forgiveness. They were kind people, well, before Temly disappeared.

It dawned on her she had no roots besides Temly. Her friend had been her only support system, and now she was gone; the wind had gone out of her sail. Where would she start? For the first time since she met Temly's family, she saw an ugliness she never realized existed. Beautiful Mrs. Cole had yelled many times and wept without reason. The cool Cole brothers didn't laugh and tease her the way they'd done before. And Mr. Cole had never been so busy he didn't acknowledge her at all.

For one more time, Asabi considered an easy way out. One she didn't overthink. Disappear.

Chapter Twenty-Four

Fela groaned, unable to contain the emotions Temly's soft body evoked.

When he'd found her naked and rescued her from those who wanted her dead, he thought she was a child, but this subtle massage of her body against his spoke otherwise. During their hikes, she'd told him her age, but he hadn't been attracted to her in a physical way. She needed help, and he was there.

Since he clocked thirteen and met Law, he'd been introduced to the opposite sex, but Temly was not his type. He liked women, not budding teenagers.

She moved again and lay spread-eagled on top of him. She was too close. Gently, so as not to wake her, he rolled to his side. It made him less aroused as well.

Soon, his urges returned. With Temly so close, he needed a cold shower—he clenched and loosed his fists. His life before now seemed like another time. Another person. What would be the harm in taking "advantage" of the girl? Yet, he found he could not. Absently, he rubbed her hip. She was pretty in her own way, and he liked her a lot when she wasn't whining.

He closed his eyes and tried to nap. Temly snuggled against him, sound asleep. The day didn't promise to be easier, and he had to find a means of providing food because the remaining biscuits wouldn't last more than a day.

He heard a dull swish of wet leaves and went still. More sounds came from outside their cover. His head pounded. His heart thumped. The machete lay with the bundle outside their wrap, and he could kick himself. If only he had it. He didn't have a weapon, only a fat stick beside him. He tightened his fingers around it and listened but heard nothing. Then he felt a slight tug as though someone nudged, testing the mound he and Temly must represent to the outside world. Something sniffed his head.

God, please.

His heart might burst from his chest. Wild animals? He wished he had a clue. He trained his nostrils but perceived nothing beyond his and Temly's scents. He prayed she would not wake. *Please, God. Send the animal away*. His palms dripped sweat. Heat he'd prayed for from the previous day's cold covered him from head to toe.

The animal moved down the length of his body and jumped on him. How many of them were there? What felt like small hooves moved over him. He waited for one of them to sink their teeth into his flesh. How could he protect Temly? Wild goats or deer? What could they be?

Their sounds told him they must have found the bundle of what little food they had left. Wild pigs. He pictured them tearing at it. If wild pigs were hungry, did they eat humans?

If he and Temly survived the night, they'd have to change direction in the light of day. Only God knew what they were in the middle of.

Temly moaned.

Not now, O Lord. Please make her dead to the world.

The animals dragged the bundle over the red cloth Fela and Temly slept under and seemed to play with it above their heads.

Temly began to stretch, and he stilled her. Together, both now fully awake, they stayed as calm as their trembling bodies allowed. The animals tried to pull the red cloth apart.

Fela prayed in the strange language his parents were fond of using during prayers. He'd never used it before and never imagined he knew how. When it didn't seem to work, he shouted at the animals to leave. Fear prevented him from coming out from under the red cloth. The animals moved off and then all went quiet.

Were they quietly watching? Were they animals at all?

He patted Temly. "Stay here. I'll check it out," he whispered.

"No, don't go. Please."

It didn't take more to persuade Fela. They remained wrapped under the cover for what seemed like ages. He couldn't summon the courage to see what had happened to the animals. He was grateful Temly didn't start crying, or he wouldn't have known what to do with her.

"I need to get out from under this blanket," he said.

Temly nodded after what seemed like forever. He lifted his head and heard nothing. He hated the silence. He stayed under the covering for several breaths and slowly removed the red cloth from his head. Dawn was breaking, and the light, though small, helped him to survey their immediate surroundings.

"What do you see?" Temly whispered from beneath.

"Look for yourself."

She sat up and pulled the cloth off. Her first reaction was to stifle a scream. The bundle was in tatters and trailed off into the darkness.

Fela stood and studied their environment. The animals were gone. Temly jumped to her feet beside him. All the biscuits were gone, eaten with their packs except for crumbs. The bottles of water were bent but still intact, and the cans of malt were untouched.

"What sort of animal eats biscuits?"

"Goats? Maybe they were wild goats."

"Could they have been bush babies?"

"Do such things exist?" Fela peered as far as he could. "Whatever they were, we are in the wrong place." This was no time for jokes, though he wanted to crack one about bush babies.

He studied the marks on the ground imprinted due to the rains of the previous day. "I think they were wild pigs or goats, but not humans."

"I heard there are communities in the hidden hills. Cannibals, too." Temly swallowed. "Please, let's leave this place."

Fela nodded and packed up what was left. There were no fresh stains today. Temly's monthly period seemed to have ceased. Fela thanked God for little mercies.

****

They decided to change direction back the way they came.

"From the rising of the sun, we have been moving toward it, heading east, right?" Fela shaded his eyes. "So we head back toward the west."

"Yes. Let's follow the sun." She hesitated. "But it means we go through those places again? The snake, and those creatures with hooves?"

He scratched his head. "You're right. Let's go north then. For a few hours, then head west."

She squirmed. "I hope we won't have gone deeper into the traps of wild animals and not find the shrine."

"We have to take the risk, Temly. We walk north for a couple of hours, turn west for a few days, and come back south."

It sounded like going in circles to her, but she couldn't offer any alternatives. "Okay," she said.

"We just have to trust our instincts." He sighed. "We don't have much of a choice."

Temly walked behind him, a myriad of thoughts running through her mind. They'd come so close to death this time. Those creatures could have been anything and done anything to them, and Fela had been strong. She admired him and realized how much she needed to be strong, too. She couldn't cry like a baby at every whim anymore.

"We will retrace our steps to the shrine, just like you suggested, then continue to walk right through."

She shuddered. "Yes. We know what the area is like so we can avoid the evil men."

After she described to him what she could about her journey to the forest, he suggested they follow the tracks from the huts where he'd found her and find the deserted market.

"Once we locate the landmarks, you know, the huts, and the market you saw, we'll be on our way to being rescued." He licked his lips. "Sound like a goal?"

She nodded. "Yeah."

He inhaled. "From the market, we can find the road."

Her mind tricked her about the night and the tingly feelings she had whenever she was close to him. All the nights they'd spent together, they'd never made any contact. He had shown her respect. Not last night.

She'd felt his touch before the intruders came though as she pretended to be asleep. Did he like her? She'd never been so close to a man before, except her brothers. She found she liked the way she felt sleeping next to him. For the first time, she was totally aware of him being close.

Asabi had been the boys' girl. All the boys in sister-schools and their social circles wanted a date with her, and Temly had found it amusing. Though she'd had one or two crushes, with Fela she felt more like a woman.

She studied his profile. He seemed distracted, resolute. Making the best of the awful circumstance they found themselves. A fly buzzed by, and he swatted the air before him with steam. She could only hope. Maybe when this was over, they could see each other again. Like on a date.

She hummed. "We can."

Chapter Twenty-Five

Asabi found the slim housekeeper, Davida, in the kitchen cooking.

Davida's long dress accentuated her curvy shape, which Asabi found a bit inappropriate for a servant. Her dark, smooth skin and well made-up face glowed.

Davida started when she walked in. "Didn't you go out with the family?"

Asabi shrugged. "I was a little sick."

"*Ah*, sorry about your health. The governor will be at the meeting this evening. It would have been good for you to be there."

"I hope everything goes well."

"You must be hungry." Davida spared her only a brief glance. "Or did you have lunch?"

"I wasn't hungry. But I am now, please."

Davida leaned in. "I'll get something for you in five minutes. Wait in the dining room."

Asabi curtsied and left. The twenty-something-year-old woman always had a pleasant disposition, unlike every other person in the household, and she was grateful for this.

She sat on one of the single chairs and waited as she'd been told. After church, where Law had stealthily pressed a key into her hand, she'd locked herself in her room, unable to decide what to do with the key. Afraid for her life and of whom to trust. Familiar feelings of fear crept over her, crippling her from action. The same fear she experienced anytime Femi Filips violated her.

Davida rushed into the dining room. "The program is on TV. Come."

They hurried into the kitchen and Asabi watched from the twenty-one-inch flat screen hung on the wall, as Pastor Peter spoke like an orator about his missing son.

"Fela has been gone for close to a week. We love him. We call for him to come home. We ask anyone with information to please come forward."

A picture of the teenager was displayed on the screen. Asabi gawked at the dark-skinned boy. His hair was cut to the scalp, and he wore a sweet smile. Clean, a poster boy.

Mama Peter's voice came up off-screen. "In God's name, we beg you. Please release our boy if you have him. We'll pay any ransom."

Other parents with missing children took turns to talk. Davida shook her head.

Asabi swallowed. "Tell me about him, their son."

"He was the black sheep. No one in this house liked him."

"He looks nice to me."

Davida snickered. "The picture was taken when he was twelve years old. He's now seventeen. Or sixteen. If you see him, you won't recognize him as the same boy."

"How do you mean?"

"He weaves his hair and wears make-up sometimes."

Asabi gasped. "What kind of boy is he?"

"He got involved with the wrong crowd." Davida frowned. "His barber friend changed him into trash."

Law? But she couldn't say his name. How would she explain it? "His barber-friend?"

"Law. He runs a brothel in his shop for gay men. Fela is one of his prostitutes."

Asabi shrunk inward. "*Oh*! But how can his parents allow this?"

Davida shrugged. "Here's your food." She placed a plate of white rice and stew on the kitchen table. "Do you want to eat here? They won't show Papa and Mama again."

"You don't think so?"

"No, they won't." Davida shook her head. "But they go to State House every day, saying the same thing, showing the same picture. Nothing will come of it."

"How sad."

Davida crossed her arms over her chest. "If you ask me, they just want the publicity. The governor told Papa to leave when he continued to preach instead of begging people to find his son."

Mabel, the plump cleaner, walked in, and Davida grabbed a pan on the cooker. Asabi took the cue and carried her food to the dining area.

After her meal, she went back to her room, conflicted. Should she help Law find his gay friend or find a way to leave, or just wait and see? One thing she knew for sure—Fela didn't have the kind of parents Temly had. His were selfish, and they used every opportunity to capitalize on their ulterior motives. It made her want to help Law find his prostitute. On the other hand, maybe the boy was better lost than found.

Chapter Twenty-Six

All the way to Calvary he went for me, he went for me, he went for me—

Temly sighed. "You've been singing this song for hours. Don't you get tired?"

"Seems to be the only one ringing in my head."

"You'll become thirsty and hungry. You should try to save your energy."

The landscape was not as thick as the forest but denser than the hillside they escaped from. Fela cut off branches and through brush when he had to, but on the whole, they found their path.

"We will stop and rest soon. I pray we can find some stones and sticks. Stone-agers made fire without being in the Boy Scouts, didn't they?" He exhaled. "I have to make a fire."

"Yes. I pray we find stones," Temly said. She prayed every other minute. Fela had used the funny language Martha used during their captivity. She would ask him about it later.

"I pray for food, too." Fela softened his voice. "In this wild bush, there will be edible plants. I pray God leads us where they are."

"Good."

"Most of all, I pray God will lead us out of here safely."

"Thank you."

Fela tugged at his shaggy hair. "You don't pray much, do you?"

After the way he'd touched her and the way she enjoyed it, talking about prayer and God seemed wrong. She felt shy, yet he hid his actions. Was it right to bring it up? He'd thought she was asleep. If she talked about it, would he hate her for pretending? Maybe he was ashamed.

Fela stopped walking. "What's with the look on your face?"

"What look?"

"Guilt. You did something you're ashamed of in church?"

Temly laughed. The first genuine one since she was kidnapped. "No, of course not."

Fela chortled. "You look like you stole meat from the cooking pot."

Maybe touching her was to indeed be a secret. Maybe he'd done more on other nights and she didn't know.

"You're thinking about something, and I'm going to get it out of you."

Temly shook her head. "How do you imagine you would?"

"I'm a magician—"

He raised his hands into the air and blew into them. He circled her three times and jumped close then tickled her, and she ran to avoid his hands. He raced after her, pulling and tickling until they both fell on the grass, laughing so hard tears came from their eyes.

"I still don't know what's bothering you." Fela smirked. "Tell me."

Temly sat up. "Sorry, my thoughts remain mine—" She gave him her back. "Look! A farm."

He jumped to his feet and pulled her up. What seemed like an abandoned field lay ahead. The high grass and thicket hid old corn stalks.

"See! Temly. We'll have food, and—civilization must be near."

Her heart leaped. "Yes. This is great."

"God answered our prayers."

She nodded. "Yes." She studied Fela. He seemed to be going through a transformation at the prospect of having his prayers answered. As a pastor's son, Temly thought it should be a normal occurrence.

"God answered." He took her hand. "Come."

He half-ran toward the field, dragging her along. Her feet hurt, but she refrained from complaining. Salvation was near. God was near. She had never experienced a miracle or a disaster before. Now she'd experienced both. None of her loved ones had ever died. The closest to evil Temly had ever known was Asabi's abuse. This newfound trust in God was sweet, though the circumstances were awful.

Couldn't God have shown her this peace at home, in the safe confines of her family walls? Things had always worked according to plan. Growing up, she depended on her father to make decisions and guide the family in the right direction. Mr. Cole was a straightforward and righteous man. As a father, he played the role, his family lacking nothing. Praying and believing God was not a visible part of Temly's childhood. Slowly, she came to the realization of the things she'd taken so much for granted; peace, progress, protection, provision. The reality shook her to the roots of her existence.

They found old corn on the cob and plucked it. They had only two bottles of water left. The canned malt drink was gone.

The weather had been fair today. Warm sunshine had dried their clothes, but the sun had set sooner than normal, and the clouds gathered again and then dispersed. Time and weather changed without consulting the two teenagers lost in the woods. Now there was just the evening coolness she was grateful for.

Fela cleared a small space under a mango tree and gathered sticks.

"I can't find any stones to make a fire."

Temly peeled the cobs. "There have to be stones here somewhere."

"*Hmm.*" Fela twitched. "Amen."

For such an abandoned farm, there had to be stones. She studied the hard corn, much too hard to be edible. Corn was in season in Ibadan. She knew because her mother loved buying fresh corn from roadside traders. For a moment, she could smell her mother's bean and corn dish, cooked with dry fish and scented leaves. Her mouth watered and she sighed. This was not the time or the place.

Fela returned with four stones. "I pray this works."

"The corn is hard, the kind farmers feed to their animals. I don't know if this can be eaten."

"We have to." He set two stones against each other and struck. One of the stones broke into pieces. "*Ahh*!" His frown stopped her from saying anything. After several tries to get a spark from the stones, he mopped sweat off his face.

"I think you should reserve your energy."

He slumped on the dirt ground beside her.

"What do we do, Lord? What do we eat tonight?" He closed his eyes. "You gave us this farm. You gave us this corn. Give us fire, Lord."

Temly didn't want to disturb his prayer, but she didn't think it would do much. She plucked a few kernels from the cob and popped into her mouth. "It's not so bad, just dry."

Fela rubbed the back of his neck. "I'm not sure it's safe to eat raw corn."

She continued to remove the seeds from the cob. "Chickens eat raw corn, and they don't die."

"Well." He took another cob and ate from it. "It tastes awful. Dry and strong. How could you chew it?"

"I have strong teeth."

"Please don't eat this. I'm not sure—God will provide something—"

"Fela, did you pray this much before? And the strange language—the woman with me, the one who was killed—she spoke it, too. Do people only speak the language when death is near? Are we going to be killed? Do you sense danger?"

He dropped the cob and pulled her close. "I'll tell you a story about the strange language." He sighed. "My father spoke it all the time. He tried to teach it to me. Forced me to speak it. He told me it was the language of the spirit of God. Told me only God understood it. Not anyone else. Not the devil."

"The woman tried to teach me. I wanted to pray with it later but couldn't remember."

"It's not taught by man. It's God's language."

Temly wanted to feel better by his explanation but couldn't. "What is God saying? Are we going to be in more trouble? Why do you keep speaking it?"

"I never took my father seriously. But now I understand it's not about the language but your ability to connect with God in your heart. The language may be a means but not the end until your heart is right."

Temly moaned. "I was worried the lady was killed despite all the strange tongues she spoke."

"Your heart and your sincerity toward God matter more than any strange language, Temly. How do I make you understand this? I feel God around here. I feel—"

The light was almost gone, and darkness beckoned. But she could see him. The look of reverence and holiness, a glow.

She feared the end was near. An end she wasn't ready for.

"I feel His presence. I did everything against God to frustrate my father. But I can't remember ever praying or singing." Tears coursed down his face. "Or loving God in my heart like this."

Temly internalized his words and all she could feel was a foreboding. Unworthiness.

"We never deserve a second chance but over and over and over again, God gave me a chance to know Him. The more my father tried to convince me, the more I pulled away."

"Do you hate your father?"

"I did." He brightened up. "But right now, I don't. I never thought it would be possible." He took her hand. "It's time, Temly. For you to turn to Jesus. If we never see another day, if we never get another chance, we'll not regret this night and the opportunity to reach out to God."

His touch this time was not like before. "Help me understand it better," she said softly.

"You need to surrender your life to God, Temly. Tomorrow may be too late."

The corn forgotten, the hunger disappeared, the fire didn't seem important. Temly felt it. It was time.

"I want to do it, Fela. Now."

Chapter Twenty-Seven

Asabi woke up early and prepared for the day. She still didn't know what to do. Temly had been the "doer" in their friendship. She was laid back, and a lot of times, until her friend pushed, she did nothing. Temly would have made up her mind by now. Though she realized by doing nothing, she was doing something—staying back with the Peters.

The night before, the man had knocked on her door again and waited longer, persuading her to come with him to the night vigil. She wanted to ask if others were attending as well, but her tongue had been glued to the roof of her mouth. Fear, like she'd known before, caused her to stay frozen in one spot. Then he'd left, and she had slept.

Another dream about her childhood horrors, more graphic than the last, made her wake up shuddering. Papa Peter had been brutal. Femi Filips, as awful as he had been, had never inflicted physical pain. The dream left her weak.

She pondered, her eyes on her suitcase. "Should I, should I not?"

Heavy footsteps from right outside her door stopped her musing. A door opened and shut, and she heard male voices.

"I am surprised you came so early," Papa Peter said.

There was a response, but Asabi didn't hear the words. She walked to her door and opened it a little. Everywhere else was quiet. It wasn't even six o'clock yet. She peeped and caught a glimpse of the back view of the two men strolling into the formal parlor.

She didn't know what she was doing, but she stepped out of her room and tiptoed toward them. Her room was the only one before a corridor opened to the parlor. There was no door but a detour, one leading to the corridor, and the other to the parlor. If anyone came toward her either way, she could escape into her room without detection. The design of the house was indescribable in an awkward way.

The other man stood in the middle of the parlor. "It's the only time I thought I could meet with you."

Papa Peter did not offer him a seat but took his elevated throne. The view resembled a king speaking to one of his subjects, but the other man stood with an air and an authority Asabi assumed wasn't one of a servant.

Peter leaned forward. "What do you want, Bishop?"

Bishop's voice was low, but intense. "Stop whatever it is you're doing. We have the hosts of Hell fighting our faith already. We don't need one of ours to join in!"

"You have no right to judge me."

"Peter, Peter! When did you become like this? When did you become this flamboyant, unapproachable little god?"

"We are gods. And because you refuse to make use of your power as such, I cannot be blamed."

"You now lack respect. You speak as though you were never a young man." Bishop paced. "What is the essence of all this?" He waved his hands around the room.

"It's the blessing of the *Most High*."

"I cringe at your use of the word, *blessing*." Bishop sighed. "What can I do to bring you back?"

"Bring me back to what?"

"To where you first believed."

"You were not a part of where I first believed. Just because I stopped attending your pastors' meetings, you think I have backslidden." Peter huffed. "So judgmental!"

"You register your vehicles with customized plate numbers. You stop traffic at odd places and odd times with your entourages. You behave so arrogantly as is unbefitting of a man of God," Bishop breathed.

"So? I choose to magnify my office any way I want!"

"What about the rumors?"

Peter stretched his back. "What rumors?"

"About your son."

He slouched back into his high seat. "*Oh*. What about it?"

"Does it not bother you what is going around in town? How you get your money?"

Peter sprang out of his seat. "What do you mean?"

Mama Peter walked in through the kitchen door on the other far side of the room, her face lit up with a wide smile. "My Lord Bishop! I heard voices and wondered who could be visiting so early."

"Good morning, madam."

"What can we offer you? Peter! You didn't ask him to sit? Welcome, sir, so glad to have you in our home."

Bishop cleared his throat. "I was just about to leave."

Peter stood. "I'll see you out." He marched toward the door, and Bishop followed him.

Asabi saw Mama Peter roll her eyes before she sneaked back into her room. What a couple. At least someone noticed they were not right and was concerned enough to speak out.

Chapter Twenty-Eight

A morning service was held to offer extensive prayers for Fela, Temly, and several other people missing from home. The state governor and his beautiful wife attended. Papa Peter recognized them and invited them to sit on the altar with him.

Asabi thought she couldn't sit through the long ritualistic service, but she had to. Several times, prayer was made for the state and the governor and his family, and at some point it seemed the program was not about the missing people, but the politicians in attendance. After three hours of a good Monday morning gone, closing prayers were said. Everyone was asked to remain seated till the governor and his entourage left.

Asabi noticed half of the full hall walk out behind the state leader. She caught sight of Law at the back of the hall and cringed. Nothing had been done about the key.

After service, she waited with the Peters' children and staff while Papa and Mama Peter had a series of meetings. Law walked to her, a frown on his face. She braced herself.

"I imagine you couldn't find a way to leave the house." He stole a look around the hall. "But it's safe here. Before they notice we're talking."

She followed his gaze. No one seemed to notice. Davida spoke with another lady down the hall, and Mabel was nowhere in sight. Gold and Diamond were bickering over something in their usual irritating manner while the toddler roamed the aisles, content to find his own entertainment. Asabi assumed their parents must have excused them from school to attend the prayers or why would kids be in church on a Monday morning in May?

"Did you use the key?"

"No."

His head snapped up. "Why?"

"Why should I? I don't know you. You can't give me orders—"

"Fela's room holds the answer to where he is. Please."

"Why are you so desperate to have him back? To continue your evil trade? Use him?"

He sneered. "What are you talking about?"

"They told me all about you. You evil man."

Law smirked. "They've won you." He chuckled. "How could I have imagined—"

Davida stomped toward the duo, a scowl on her face. "It's time to go home."

Asabi picked up her purse.

"Until you do what I say, you won't be free." Law walked away.

Davida cleared her throat. "Evil man. What was he telling you?"

Asabi gazed after him and sighed. Davida seemed nice to talk to, but she didn't know much about her either. One of her weaknesses was talking to people. She'd rather be quiet and watch, wait. Her curiosity about Law increased.

"Don't listen to him," Davida said. "This is what he did to Fela until the poor boy became something else."

Asabi licked lips gone dry. She couldn't listen to Law and listen to Davida. Many questions danced in her head.

"What did he want you to do, anyway?"

"Open Fela's room." She didn't think anything of it because she didn't for one moment believe Law. If he could turn a normal teenager to a gay prostitute, he was worse than Femi Filips. Yet, she wished she could believe him.

"What! Why does he want you to?" Davida's exclamation drew attention from few members still in the hall. "This man is so evil. Are you sure he didn't ask you to do any other thing?"

Asabi nodded. "Yes." Had she said too much?

Davida shook her head. "Law should be stoned. He is so evil."

"But—" Asabi shrugged. "What's in Fela's room?"

"Let's go home. Come on."

Davida ushered her and the children out, and they rode with a driver in silence. She wished the older woman would tell her the mysteries around Fela and his family. Her curiosity was pricked. But she couldn't find the courage to ask.

After lunch, everyone retired into their rooms. Asabi paced, unable to decide what she should do. But she had to leave. She hadn't done anything here to help Temly.

She'd wasted her time here. Inhaling, she grabbed Law's key. On her way out, she'd tell Mama Peter she needed to go back home and then return the key to Law before she left town.

Her quest to find her biological father was still solid in her mind. She would pursue it later. But first she had to find Temly. Somehow. She flung her bag over her shoulder, ensured she left nothing, closed her eyes for a moment, and took another deep breath.

She opened her door and walked to the parlor. Then the kitchen. No one was in sight. She had to bid them farewell. It would be wrong to just leave. Besides, the security man at the gate would not let her go without an explanation.

Down the corridor, harsh, whispery voices stopped her. She recognized them as Davida's and Mama Peter's. A curiosity she hadn't known she possessed pushed her toward the conversation. She moved on tiptoes like she did early in the morning; she considered this would be the only way to get any truth in this house. Eavesdropping.

"You've come a long way to allow him to treat you like this." Davida snorted. "And I'm tired of pretending to be your servant."

"Don't talk like this, Davida. Time will make everything right."

"Time I'm tired of. When will you gather enough money to leave him? He treats you like you don't exist, and you let him."

"He knows I'm not a fool."

"I'm not sure. I'm not sure at all. This pretense has gone on for too long. At least free me. Give me some money. Let me go back to Lagos and start my life over. You brought me here so my life would change—"

"And has it not? Davida? Are you still working the streets, taking strangers into your body? Smoking and—?"

"*Shh*, Nkiru. Someone might hear you. You don't even fear. See how you're talking. We had the same life. You got lucky and married a man of God—"

Asabi scrunched her nose. Who was Nkiru? Was there a third person with them? She pinched herself. It had to be the pastor's wife's name.

Mama Peter laughed. "Don't deceive yourself. Not even for one day."

"I wonder how people follow him around and not suspect."

"People are foolish. And Favor Peter has perfected the art of deceit."

Asabi heard a sound, like the rustling of clothes. It was so quiet she couldn't breathe.

"He's good. Even I get carried away sometimes."

"His evil powers work on you then."

Asabi flattened her back against the wall. Goosebumps rose on her arms and face. She shuddered at the thought of being caught here, but she was afraid to move, afraid they'd hear.

"Get me five million naira. I can leave and start a life for myself in Lagos."

"What about me? We had a deal."

"And the deal has gone on for too long. Seventeen long years! Look at me, living here like a housemaid. I want to get married, have children like you. See Nkiru, I'm not getting any younger. You're just two years older than me, but it looks like twenty. If our mother was alive, she'd disown you for treating me like this."

Mama Peter stifled a snort. "Thank God Mama died long ago." The rustling sound again. "Davida, please, give me a little more time. I've gathered ten million, ten more and we can both leave. Do you think I want to be in his house, living like this after you're gone?"

Davida sighed. "Do you think he knows you've been stealing from him?"

"Even if he knows, he hasn't said anything about it," Mama Peter whispered. "He's too afraid I will expose his secrets."

"If so, I don't think we're safe. Let's take what you've gathered and go. Take the children tonight and leave him for good."

Mama Peter chuckled. "You have ideas."

"I'm just tired of this lifestyle. Seeing him gives me the creeps."

"We will survive."

Asabi heard a patting sound and then silence. More rustling noise came through the door. She straightened. She had to leave. She contemplated getting the door.

Davida's voice came out in a scratchy stutter. "Do you think he killed Fela?"

What expression would be on Mama Peter's face? She'd expect anger and hurt and frustration.

"I believe so."

Asabi shut her eyes. She couldn't listen anymore. She tiptoed to the parlor, picked up her luggage, and ran back to her room, shivering from head to toe.

She wished she'd never found these people.

Chapter Twenty-Nine

Fela shared a bottle of water with Temly in the morning.

After the celestial experience the night before, he was in high spirits. He gloried in the things God had done and trusted He would do more. They were on a journey to wherever He took them. He wasn't afraid anymore, and Temly followed his lead.

With the supplies gone, Fela carried the red cloth and Temly the bottle of water. With no food in their stomachs, their trek was slow and by the time the sun came up high and hot, she struggled to walk upright.

"We'll stay a little and rest." He spread the red cloth under a tree with many branches, and they both sat. He was worried Temly wouldn't be able to continue. She had to be strong, yet he wished he could help her in some way.

"I'm so hungry. Has God forgotten us so soon?" Temly moaned. "After last night, I thought—"

"God works in mysterious ways, Temly. He knows what's best."

She bit on her lower lip. "Then what's best? Hunger?"

"He who watches Israel neither sleeps nor slumbers—"

"*Huh*, there you go again with your scriptures."

"Are you discouraged so fast?" He clenched his jaw. "Last night, you were excited and full of the spirit of God." Could last night have been a fantasy, a product of his imagination? He hated to think it.

"Because I thought you knew what you were doing. I thought God was speaking to you!"

"Yes, God was speaking—"

"Well, what did he say?"

Fela got on his feet. "He didn't tell me He would get food for us today. He didn't even tell me He would save us from death. But He does promise eternal life." He walked away.

Perhaps too weak for a fight, Temly didn't call him to stop or follow. He walked several meters until he couldn't see her anymore but just a bit of the red blanket. He couldn't lose sight of her, but he needed to pray.

"This is where I am, Lord. Give us food. If only for one, for Temly, so she will not lose faith in You. Help us, Lord. Do what only You can do."

His stomach rumbled and twisted painfully. At this point, he would eat fresh leaves if he were sure they weren't poisonous. The corn would have worked if it had been edible. It must have been planted the previous year. If so, why hadn't it rotted or been eaten by birds?

He stared up at the clear blue sky. "If You are there, and I have found You, and You saved me from my wretched existence, from all the terrible things I did. If You are God, give us food—"

He didn't know how long he stayed on his knees on the same spot, but he heard Temly behind him.

"I hear sounds. I couldn't stay alone."

His heart warmed up to her. "Come. I've been praying and I hope it's God's voice I heard and not my hungry gut."

"God's voice? How do you hear it?"

"In my heart. He said we should look at the trees."

Her right arm held the other at the elbow. "The weather is changing again. Should we stay here or move on?"

He didn't think she believed him, but he knew what he'd heard, and he wanted to obey. He walked in circles, gazing at the trees.

Temly observed the clouds. "Maybe we'll find some fruits, or He plans to rain manna." Though she didn't go to church much, she knew some Bible stories.

"No, Temly." He took her hand and ran to the tree they'd slept under. "Look up." He did, and she did too. The tree was leafy.

Temly pressed her lips together. "I can't see anything but leaves."

He couldn't see anything either. Were the leaves edible? What did the instruction mean? He'd heard it as clear as if it were Temly who spoke. *God please, honor Your word,* he prayed quietly.

"Look closer. Do you see anything?" Temly said.

His gaze followed her pointing finger. "Guava, I think. It looks bigger than any I've seen." A sob escaped his lips. "Thank You, God."

He could see only one, but he'd prayed as long as Temly could eat something.

"We need a stick. The fruit is so high up."

"I will climb."

Temly touched his hand. "Be careful."

Fela reached for a low limb. He climbed with energy he didn't know he had, and within seconds, was close to the guava. "I'll toss it down." Something crawled up his arm and he swatted it off just in time. "Ants! Giant ants, Temly, roll up the blanket. Quick."

"Maybe you should just come down."

Fela laughed. "No way." He used his machete to cut off a branch.

Temly saw the branch fall with a throng of ants, and quickly caught up the blanket.

Fela threw the big guava and it landed with a thud. "Catch."

Temly yelped. "Thank You, God."

"I see another one. Steer clear. The ants will fall with the branches."

"Yes, sir."

It occurred to him to cut more branches. As he cut them, he found the big guavas hidden among the leaves. A black ant stung him on the cheek, sending burn sensations to his brain, and he closed his eyes in a spontaneous reaction. He swiped at it but realized the gesture was futile as more ants landed on his head and crawled over him.

"We have ten, Fela. Come down. I'm afraid you'll fall."

"Let me check for more. More is better, right?" He found two more and climbed down.

Temly screamed when she saw his face and hands covered in insect bites. "They attacked you. Why didn't you just come down? Do they hurt?" She tried to touch his face, but he stepped back.

"They itch like the devil but not so painful." He wiped sweat from his face. "I have an idea. Bring the red blanket." He spread branches on the ground and put the red cloth on them, then covered it with more branches.

"What are you doing?"

"I think it'll rain. I hope the branches will keep the blanket dry."

She picked the two biggest guavas. "God provided food. They're not hard. And not too soft either." She sank her teeth into one. "It's white, and not a lot of seeds!"

Fela laughed. "God is faithful."

They ate two each and chatted about fruits and how their parents had once forced them to eat.

"I've never seen guavas this big. I thought I would die of hunger today." Temly's eyes twinkled. "Thank you."

"I've never seen a guava tree. Thank God." He sighed. "He never fails."

The cloud emptied its bowels on them. Fela carved a few leaves to form a hollow to collect water and filled the empty bottle after they'd had a drink. When the rain subsided, they walked a little distance away from each other and squeezed water from their clothes.

They found the red cloth dry as though rain had not fallen, and this kept them a little warm through the rest of the day and night.

The guavas would last another day then Fela shut out the thought of the morrow. He would not succumb to fear after hope had been rekindled. He struggled not to think about the horrible insect bites on his body or the insane urge to scratch them.

If the stings were poisonous, he could die in this forest.

Chapter Thirty

A week ago today, everything changed.

Asabi couldn't believe how slow time passed. It seemed like years since she'd laughed and joked with Temly. When their lives seemed normal and nothing unfamiliar disturbed their space. Except Femi Filips. Was God punishing her for letting Femi abuse her all these years?

She opened her luggage and brought out her photo album. She plucked at the pictures she took before Femi Filips came into their lives and sniffed away tears. Ten years ago, they'd met while she and Temly bought sweets in his pharmacy and insisted on meeting their parents. She had thought he was a nice man who took genuine interest in her and her family.

When he found her father didn't live with them, he became Daddy to her. He'd so loved, so doted on her. She'd thought her mother loved and married him for it. This was ten years ago. Today, she thought differently. Her mother had never loved Femi Filips. She only married him for his wealth, or she should have left him the first time she caught him with her.

Before Femi came into their lives, she had been a cheerful five-year old. Her mother said she had no secrets, rebuked her often for being so loud and stubborn. After the first encounter with Femi, when he stole what was most precious to her, Asabi's sparkle died.

She closed the album, her chest constricted with pain. But she didn't cry because Davida knocked on her door.

"We're going for evangelism. Do you wish to join us?"

Asabi sniffed and composed herself. "*Huh*, what time is it now—I'm sorry." She opened the door. "I'm sorry."

"For what?" Davida narrowed her eyes. "What were you doing?"

"Just thinking about Temly." She pressed her fingers to her lips. "I'm sorry."

"*Oh*, poor girl." Davida shrugged. "They'll find her."

"Amen."

"I'll tell them you want to stay at home and pray for Temly and Fela."

"Thank you."

When Davida left, Asabi closed the door and sighed. She didn't want to be here, yet she couldn't find the courage to leave. Something held her back. A strange power she couldn't control. To discover Davida and Mama Peter had a secret between them made her miserable. Thinking about what she'd overheard caused her to pale inside.

Since the day before, she'd considered telling Davida she knew her secret. She felt guilt for hearing them. But would it not jeopardize her stay in the house? She was confused. She wished Temly were with her. What would Temly do?

She walked to her window and watched the family leave in two Jeeps. On Sunday night, confession night as they called it, Papa Peter had made her confess her sins and "receive" the Lord to save her soul. The singular act qualified her to be a part of the spiritual family and able to go for evangelism. Whatever it meant.

The thought of returning Law's key occurred to her. She could tell the security guard she was asleep when the family left and she wanted to join in the evangelism.

A quick brush of her hair made her presentable. She picked up her bag and stopped at a thought.

What was the harm in checking Fela's room if no one was home? She could look through quickly and then return the key. It wasn't likely she'd find anything.

She took a deep breath and found the girls' room, then Olive's. Another room was not locked, but when she opened it, a mysterious feeling overwhelmed her, and she slammed it shut. Odd, because it was empty.

Two rooms were locked. Which belonged to Fela?

She tried the key in one and it opened. But when she entered, she discovered it was the master bedroom. Curiosity urged her to stay in the massive room. It wasn't the room she'd heard Davida and Mama Peter talk from the other day. This room was closer to the parlor, next to the girls' room, and it bespoke wealth.

A king-size bed occupied the middle of the room, covered with a gold embroidered duvet. Floor-to-ceiling mirrors lined the wall facing the bed, and a massive dresser punctuated it with cosmetics and perfumes, enough for five flamboyant women. Asabi peeped into a walk-in wardrobe and saw rows and rows of neatly arranged clothes on hangers and shoes on racks. She couldn't see the end of the wardrobe.

Papa and Mama Peter's bedroom, she assumed.

Another door to the bathroom was ajar and Asabi saw a part of a Jacuzzi. A huge television screen was placed at an odd angle on the wall. How would they watch it if they lay on the bed? Except if they dragged one of the three leather couches placed at each corner of the room closer.

She touched the edge of the bed. It was hard, and she wondered why it should be. She'd heard of the orthopedic mattress from her step-grandmother who Femi Filips ensured she visited often. Who between the couple had a bad back? She sat and then lay on it. So hard.

This was so wrong, she knew, but for a moment, she wanted to hurt these people who were so phony and selfish. Who would let a barber take over the life of their son and probably kill him? Had Mama Peter said she thought Papa Peter killed Fela? What mother would be so calm after such a revelation? Even Eni Filips, despite being such a bad mother—Asabi sighed. At least Temly's mother remained a good example to her.

She opened the drawers at the bureau and found some cash. What if she took it? It was a lot of money in wrapped bundles of one-thousand-naira bills. The woman had been stealing from her husband, but would taking her money be the right thing to do to punish her? Who cared? Her husband didn't.

Asabi walked to the door. This wasn't right. No matter how awful these people were, she had no right to look through their private room. She was an intruder, and guilt made her step out, careful to lock the door.

How did Law have the key to the room? Or could the key open all doors in the house? This piqued her interest even more.

Chapter Thirty-One

The key opened the second locked door as well. Fela's room!

A life-size portrait of the boy, his hair heaped high on his head, his face made-up, with his shirt open to the waist, and tight jeans slashed at ungodly places, hung on the wall facing the door. His muscles bulged, and Asabi thought he was good-looking.

For a moment, her breath hitched, she stood frozen. Fela glowered at whoever stood at his door, one eyebrow arched, his even white teeth sunk into his lower lip, his hand hooked in his belt riding low on his hip.

Asabi closed the door and searched the room. A strong male scent mixed with muskiness accosted her, and she gasped. The queen-size bed was rumpled like someone had just awakened from it. Shoes, clothes, and other personal items were scattered on the floor and on every surface in the room like the owner hadn't a care for them.

She stepped around underwear and belts. She didn't know what to look for. What clues could be here? She wished she could call Law and ask him where to look, but she didn't have his number. And didn't trust him so much.

She opened the closet and gingerly touched Fela's clothes dumped in a messy heap. It didn't feel right to touch his—things. Asabi simpered at the thought of straightening the clothes. How absurd, but she did it in hopes of finding—she didn't know what.

Done with the closet and no interesting discovery, she checked under his bed and found lots of junk. Nothing important in the bathroom either.

She walked to the door and examined the room once more. His table. Okay. She picked up his schoolbooks, littered all over. Nothing important except a diary.

Asabi opened it and for the next half an hour, consumed the most thrilling tales about Fela's life in his voice, his handwriting.

****

"Papa says no one is going out—" the gateman said before she could speak.

"I'm going for evangelism. I was asleep when they left. I don't know why they didn't wake me."

The man hesitated and then opened the gate. Asabi gave him a nod and walked off, her Bible clutched in her embrace. The big Bible had been a gift from Papa Peter after she was led to the Lord. She'd been given passages to read since and asked to explain what she read. She wondered why the security at the gate was so tight. As a visitor, why couldn't she come and go as she pleased?

She took a taxi, and as Law had advised, told the driver to take her to Law's barbershop. The ride was not a long one, which surprised Asabi. Did Law truly commit these atrocities against a pastor's son so close to home?

The barbershop was located on the end of a long line of small shops. Asabi approached with caution. She imagined young men in skirts with long hair and make-up. Through a window, she could see Law sat alone on a stool close to a corner of the shop. On the window was the sign: *"Sorry, We're Closed."*

Asabi knocked, and Law glanced up. His eyes were bloodshot, and his dreadlocks a tangled mess. He opened to her, his features softened by the hope she could read in his eyes.

"I've prayed all day you'd come."

"I'm on my way out of town. I thought it was only fair to try what you asked."

He pointed at her bag. "You came with only a handbag?"

"I had to stuff important things in here. My suitcase will have to stay behind."

He raked his hair. "Please, come in. Have a seat." He walked to a small fridge. "Can I offer you something to drink?"

She took one of several plastic visitors' chairs. "No, thank you. It's getting late, and I want to return to Ibadan today."

He checked his watch. "It's too late to go to Ibadan. I can put you in a hotel, and you can leave tomorrow morning."

It was a generous offer. But he was a stranger. "Thanks, but no. I can take care of myself."

He shrugged. "Did you find anything in Fela's room?"

"Yes." She opened her bag and brought out the diary. "Here."

He grabbed it like an urchin a piece of dry bread. "Thank you."

"I read part of it. He writes like a poet." She scratched a spot on her neck. "But he wrote some with a code."

Law opened the diary to the last few pages; his gaze pored over every line. He flipped to the last page and closed the diary.

"May I know?" Asabi shrugged. "Of course, it's none of my business but—"

"The day Fela went missing, he was here with me. We discussed something important. I feared he would be hurt."

"Okay."

"There is a room in his house, which we thought was strange. He wanted to enter the room. I was afraid something evil would happen and I pleaded with him not to." Law held up the diary. "He promised to write about it in his diary."

"Can you read what he wrote?"

"We have this code. We use it all the time. *Ca4da2.*"

Asabi shook her head. "I saw a lot of this throughout the diary, but he wrote simple English, too."

"I'll teach you how to decode it someday but first, we have to find Fela. Please. Can I ask you not to leave tonight?"

Asabi stood. "No way. I'm done with the house and all those weird people in it. Besides, today marks one week since my friend disappeared." Tears came to her eyes. "I don't know what I'm doing here. I haven't made any progress towards finding her. I have to leave."

"Fela disappeared a week ago, too. From what I read in his diary, he entered the room. I feared he wouldn't come out, but he said he did." Law opened the diary and stood beside Asabi. "Look."

"*3 2nata2ra2da 1nada da3dana'ta sa22 ma2. Da1da—*"

"What does it mean?" Asabi touched her forehead. "Just tell me, please."

"It reads: *I entered and didn't see me. Dad came in, too. I don't think he saw me. I have to follow him tonight. He's going for a night vigil, and I don't think its church. I must follow him. Tonight.*" Law pressed his lips together.

"He followed his father and never came back." Asabi covered her mouth. "*Wow*. He knows where Fela is. *Wow*."

What kind of father was this? Asabi thought of the massive pretense in the Peters' family. She thought she'd come from a dysfunctional home. But hers was like child's play compared to this.

"A night vigil."

"Do you know anything about it?"

"He has knocked on my door every night since I arrived, asking me if I wanted to go for the night vigil with him."

Law leapt to his feet. "And what did you say?"

"He scares me. He looks through people. I've not given him a response. He normally came to knock on my door after everyone had gone to sleep. I just stay quiet and say nothing."

"You see why I need you to stay? Please." Law's lips trembled. "If he asks you tonight, will you follow him? Please?"

Chapter Thirty-Two

Asabi stood from her bed and stretched.

She checked her cell phone for the time, even though her alarm woke her. Law had told her things to look for in Fela's room, and much as she hated to continue, she pitied him. He seemed concerned for Fela. She understood him. It was just the way Temly felt about her. Everyone needed a friend, and if she had Temly, then no matter what kind of pervert Fela was, he deserved at least one person who understood him. Law.

So she agreed to stay and do what she could to help. Law's excitement over the diary made her stop to think again about her choices. He'd taught her the code. Every vowel was represented as a number, and each consonant had the letter "a" added after it. She was amazed at it. Perhaps if she'd done this, she'd have been able to communicate easier with Temly and her friend wouldn't have gone missing.

Asabi walked into the bathroom and had a quick shower. It was still early but in a couple of hours, the house would come awake. She wanted to be out of Fela's room by then.

Law planned to go to the police with the information in Fela's diary. The boy had indicated he was going with his father for the night vigil. Law was afraid the diary alone wouldn't cause the police to question Fela's father. Such a father! If Femi Filips was a monster, then Papa Peter was a dragon.

She had been angry with him for suggesting she follow the evil pastor to the night vigil. What if it was true and it was just a trap to kill people? Nothing he said made sense, but she hadn't been able to reject his plea for her to stay longer and get some of Fela's pictures from the photo album in his closet to back up the evidence he was gathering against Papa Peter.

She'd come to find help for Temly, but if all she accomplished were to help find Fela, then she'd be satisfied. Beyond doubt, Papa Peter knew where Fela was and lied about the kidnapping. Asabi shuddered at the mere thought. Did Mama Peter know about this? Was she also caught in this wickedness and deceit? And Davida, the only seeming human in the household, was she also a part of this? Mama Peter was not a good wife to her husband, deceiving and stealing from him, but was there more?

Weakened by the truths she faced, Asabi sat on the bed, still tied in her towel, and buried her head in her hands. What was she to do? If she got the album for Law, then what? Could she walk away? Go back to Ibadan to her family and Temly's? What if Temly was never found? How would she ever get on with her life?

She thought of her father, whom she'd never met. Could he help? Would he even want to see her? She'd managed to contact him again. He'd told her he was in Lagos at the fixed time, but she should fix another time to meet him whenever she was ready. Should she forget about the Peters and Law and Temly and just follow through with her original plan? Disappear from everyone's radar and start her life fresh with her father?

She'd made no progress in finding Temly. Instead she'd gotten embroiled in a messy family issue. Why not leave this all behind?

She had two options: one, go back to Temly's family and apologize. They would take her back. Of course, they'd be suspicious of where she'd been and angry, but they loved her. She was sure. The other option was to go to Lagos to find her father. He might help with the search. Asabi knew little about him and had only found him a few months back. He had only one silhouetted picture online, and nothing more. She couldn't recognize him unless he introduced himself. He'd seemed cautious in his messages. What could he be afraid of? Or did he have another family? Maybe he was just being polite by replying to her messages. She'd learned people aren't always what they present to be.

She fell back on the cool sheets and sobbed. "God, if You exist, where are You? Where is Temly? What am I doing here? What do I do now?"

Her tears refreshed her. When she straightened, she knew what she had to do. Law needed help, and if she could give it, then she would. She took a deep breath and dressed. She had to have a clear mind. She would take the album to Law and return to Ibadan. She didn't need any more complications in her life. She would commit the rest of her life to finding Temly, the most important reason for her to be strong.

Someone knocked aloud and she jumped.

"Asabi!" It was one of the Peter girls. "My mom wants you now."

Asabi suspected it to be Gold, the older one. She could be so rude. The only person she feared was her abnormal father, and even he at times got a piece of her badmouthing when he didn't notice.

What did Mama Peter want with her?

"Okay, I'm coming."

The girl banged on the door again. "Come now!"

Asabi stepped out of her room and found Gold, her plump arms folded across her chest with her mouth in a pout. She was just a year younger but behaved more superior. Her baby fat didn't look like it would disappear soon, and she wore clothes not age-appropriate. She dressed like a baby doll. A fat one, though. Asabi was a few inches taller, much slimmer and ladylike, a mile prettier, and she enjoyed knowing Gold didn't like it one bit. After seeing Fela's taut physique and good looks, though, she thought Gold may have hope to be pretty if she took better care of herself.

Gold gave her a once-over. "Have you had your bath?"

Asabi nodded.

"Good. Mom wants you in her room now. It's all the way down the corridor. At the end." She stomped off.

Asabi knew the room. Had been inside, touched stuff. She hated the guilt.

Chapter Thirty-Three

Asabi knocked on the door and entered the room when prompted. The mount of clothes on the huge orthopedic bed, heaped to one side while Diamond lay sprawled and asleep on the other side caught her attention first. Davida spared her a moment before she returned to her task in the closet.

Mama Peter's eyes were puffy like she'd been up for hours.

Asabi clasped her hands. "Good morning, Mama Peter."

"*Ah*, Asabi, good morning. Come in. Come," she summoned with a high-pitched voice. "We are going for a charity march with the governor this morning to fight against kidnapping and all other forms of crime in the state."

Asabi took a tentative step toward the older woman, wondering what this had to do with her.

"Help me fold those clothes on the bed. It's going to be great. I think your friend's uncle is doing the same in Oyo State." Mama Peter addressed Davida. "I hear an international news channel may be covering the events."

Davida exclaimed, "How wonderful, indeed. Maybe they'll interview you and Papa."

"Papa is counting on it. Do you know the kind of platform it will give the ministry?"

"We will move from the stadium to the state motherless babies' home, and then to General Hospital, then prison. And we will give away these items." Mama Peter waved. "By the time they see what we are bringing, they will let us sit with the governor at the final rally in the government house."

Davida raised an eyebrow. "Have you chosen what to wear? You need to kill it."

The two deceptive sisters continued to talk about the event with so much enthusiasm Asabi cringed. This had nothing to do with a missing son or helping those in need. For them, it was an opportunity to show off.

On the other hand, she didn't want to be seen on any news platform, international or not, doing a charity walk or whatever. The Coles may watch and see her. The mere thought made her shudder. Tunji had called several times, but she'd refused to take his call or return them. After the simple text message apologizing for her actions, she hadn't been in touch.

Gold walked in and snapped with a loud voice about something Asabi wasn't familiar with. Her voice startled her sister.

Mama Peter hissed, not intimidated by her older daughter's grudge. "Gold, will you help Asabi finish folding the clothes?"

Gold rolled her eyes. "She's been on it since?"

Asabi picked one of the clothes she had to fold. She couldn't be on TV.

Gold held up a beautiful red dress and exclaimed. "Mom! Are you giving this pretty dress, too?" She pouted. "I asked you for it!"

"It's all torn at the sides, dear. You won't want it anymore."

Davida snickered. "And you're too fat for it anyway."

"Please, this is not your business, Davida. You're just a servant."

Davida moved toward Gold, but Mama Peter stopped her with a steely call, "Davida! Face your work."

There were a few minutes of silence before Papa Peter walked in and hurried the women. Within the next hour, everyone was assembled in the lobby, ready to depart. Asabi couldn't think of what to say, or how to avoid this outing.

Mama Peter nudged her forward once they arrived at the meeting point. "You will stand beside me."

Asabi breathed hard. Could she feign some form of sickness? Once upon a time she could puke with a finger in her throat, but everyone had been told breakfast would be at the state house after the charity walk. She didn't have even water in her stomach.

She walked up to Davida. "I need to use the loo."

Davida puckered her brow. "Now?"

"Yes." She pressed her thighs. "I have to go fast."

"There's nowhere here." Davida sighed. "See, Mama is waving at you to come over. The governor has arrived."

"Please. I'll find a bush somewhere close."

Both examined the surroundings and there were houses on both sides of the road. Still, Asabi dashed off, unsure of where she'd go next. More people had gathered, and security personnel on the governor's payroll filled everywhere. She stole a glance toward the front of the crowd and noticed Mama Peter looking around trying to find her.

A hand gripped her arm and pulled her. She gasped at her assailant. "Law."

He whispered, "Did you get it?"

She shook her arm out of his grip. "No. Let go."

"You were supposed to—"

"And I couldn't." She stepped away but remembered her plight. "I don't want to be on TV. My parents don't know I'm here."

"Come with me." He led the way, and she followed.

"I don't want to be lost."

"You're safe with me."

"I still need to get back."

"I know."

She stopped walking after him. "Then where are we going?"

"We'll maintain a safe distance and meet them at the state house afterwards. They won't see you until the show is over."

Asabi heaved. "Good. Thank you."

Chapter Thirty-Four

Asabi returned to her room breathless, after sneaking down the corridor to be sure everywhere was quiet and double-checked to confirm her things were all packed. This time, she carried her suitcase. The security man would query her, but she had a plan. She would feign she needed to throw out the trash. She hoped there was some to throw out and he wouldn't notice her luggage.

She crept through the kitchen and found the bin. There was trash. She tied the garbage-bag and carried it out the back. Then she went to Fela's room for his album.

Asabi heard Mama Peter's voice down the corridor, praying. Good for her. Evil people. They had been mad at her the day before, after she disappeared at the beginning of the rally only to resurface at the end. Her simple reason was she'd gone to find a bathroom and lost her way. Still, they yelled at her.

She unlocked Fela's door and slid in. She walked to his life-size portrait and touched it. *Law will find you. Or at least bring your father to justice. I know.*

She liked what she knew of him. Though the horrible black eyeliner and red lipstick did his good looks no justice, she felt only compassion. For a moment, she wondered at the relationship he had with Law. Though it bothered her, the older man seemed caring. How could he deprave Fela in such a way? He was old enough to be Fela's father, but was this the substitute he could give the boy to replace his deceptive, spiritual father?

Asabi wished, for Fela's sake, she could stay longer and help follow through with the search or Law's plan, but she didn't have such luxury. A certain sense of urgency caught her. She *had* to get back to Ibadan.

Maybe it was intuition. Maybe Temly had been found. She didn't have the courage to call and find out, but she had to return.

Asabi had seen the album on her first visit to Fela's room. She found it again and, out of curiosity, leafed through the pages. Fela seemed to be an articulate young man. Each page was labelled with dates and names of the people in the pictures. He'd been such a beautiful baby, and there were many pictures of him in the early days of his life. Asabi could imagine how his parents had expected so much from him.

Overwhelmed by the tenderness within her, she sat on the floor facing the wardrobe she had just got the album from and continued to pore over the pages. His first few days on earth, with Mama Peter smiling wearily. There were pictures from each of his birthdays.

Asabi saw the picture displayed on TV; the one Davida said was taken when Fela was about twelve. From then on, the transformation began. There were a few pictures with his longer hair.

Just like pictures she'd seen of the American pop legend, Fela's transformation had been in stages. Seeing it tore at Asabi's heart. How could such an innocent boy become—something like this?

She flipped the page and saw a letter. It was addressed to God and written in Fela's hand. Asabi read it, and tears gathered in her eyes. She tucked the letter back into the page and flipped to the next.

This was what Law was probably looking for. Fela spoke the deepest truths in his heart to a God she still found hard to accept. If God were there, why did he allow so much evil on earth? Fela seemed to ask the same questions.

"If you exist, God, show Yourself to me. Take me out of here and show Your power to me. I hate my father and my mother. I hate knowing they hate me. Take me out of here—"

Asabi clutched her chest and stifled her sobs. The things we wish for sometimes become our undoing. Fela was out of here now, just as he'd prayed to God, but most likely dead. Well, Law wanted to fight for him — dead or alive.

Asabi couldn't look through anymore. Tears blurred her vision, and she swallowed. His story was a tragedy if ever she had read one. She could identify with a mean and perverted stepfather. She could walk away from such a person. How would it feel to have such a man as your father? Asabi couldn't comprehend it. All the years she had fantasized about being with her father were based on the image Temly's presented. Surely fathers were kind and caring and would never hurt their children. Not Fela's father. To what end, she couldn't understand.

She had to go. The pain here was more than what she'd had in her life. She pushed herself up and wiped the tears from her face. She would give the album to Law and dust her feet from this city. She had failed Temly in some way, and she prayed she would one day make up for it. For now, she needed to leave this house and city and run as far as wherever her father would meet her.

She spun around and bumped into Papa Peter. She screamed and the album dropped with a loud thud.

Chapter Thirty-Five

Papa Peter bent and picked up the album.

Asabi stepped back, afraid of what he might do to her.

"*Shh*. You will wake the whole city." He moved in front of her and blocked her view of the door. Any hope of a quick escape vanished. "What is this?"

Asabi studied him while her heart hammered against her chest. "I was curious."

"Curiosity killed the cat." He gave a creepy smile. "And you should be well on your way, my dear."

"I'm sorry, sir. I'll pack my things and leave your house." She moved toward him to escape.

He blocked her advance. "No, I don't want you to go." He drew attention to Fela's album. "Let's look at it together."

He gripped Asabi's upper arm with such force she winced. He made her sit on the bed and sat next to her. What could she do? She prayed. *God please save me from this monster.*

He opened the album and ogled her. "Fela was such a beautiful baby boy. Don't you agree?"

"Please let me go, sir."

"Answer me!"

She recoiled. "I only wanted to know more about your son. I didn't mean to snoop."

Papa Peter opened to the next page and the next. "But you are snooping. And you are lying." He raised her chin and seemed to look through her. "Your soul has not been delivered from Hell. Your spirit is still dead to God." He shook his head. "You are of no eternal value to the kingdom."

Tears streamed down her face. Something about being so close to him choked her. How could one man carry such a frightful presence? She didn't understand what he meant, but the hairs at her nape stood, and goose bumps covered her arms.

"Please don't hurt me. I will do anything you say."

Papa Peter laughed. "Not your place to decide." He flipped several more pages. "*Ah*, when he started school." He traced his fingers over Fela's face. "He was the most brilliant until—" He squinted and went through more pages.

Asabi swallowed and prayed again. She was scared her pleading would annoy this man, but she was so afraid. Although she'd found him creepy from the start, some of her fears were based more on Law's disgust for the man, and Law was biased. He believed Papa Peter was evil. She could believe it, too, but it wasn't from anything he'd done to her. Only the dreams, this feeling—and the statements inferred when she eavesdropped, along with the attitude toward their missing son, which didn't sit well with her.

She tried to relax and paid attention to her captor.

"*Oh*, he has this picture. Silly boy."

Asabi stared at the twelve-year-old Fela. "It's the same picture you used for his search."

An apparition of a smile touched Papa Peter's eyes. "It was the last sane picture he took." His voice hardened. "Before the devil possessed him. Which other picture will one use in the media? Who in the world will help you find a boy with looks like—this?" He waved at the portrait.

"Why didn't you cast the demon from him, sir?"

"I have." He came to the page with the wall poster picture. "Indeed, I have." Two more pages afterwards with Fela dressed in outfits suggesting his new weird lifestyle, and then he came to the page with the letter.

Asabi's lips trembled. Should she discourage him from reading it or not? Then he'd know she'd already read it. She watched Papa Peter read the hate-letter describing Fela's parents as evil monsters and how he wished to leave.

He folded the letter back. "He got his wish," he mumbled.

He opened the next page of the album, and there was another letter. Asabi had not seen this. She wished she hadn't been such a coward and had taken the album and run.

The man of God read this, too. "He will have his wish!"

Papa Peter jumped to his feet and heaved Asabi up. "Not only will he die, all his friends will die with him." He pushed Asabi toward the door. "You think I don't know you? Law sent you to come into the house and feign a stranger. You are one of them, aren't you?"

Asabi pooled her inner instinct to survive and straightened. "No, sir."

She was just a few feet from the door. If only she could get the handle, she'd be gone before he could grab her. But he shoved her harder, and she hit her face against the solid panel door. A shout of pain escaped her lips. Blackness fought to overtake her, and the door doubled in her sight. She reached for one of the handles but caught air.

Papa Peter whirled her around and pressed her back against the wall. He slapped her several times on both sides of her face, leaving her gasping for breath.

He then held her shoulders and banged her against the wall until she became dizzy. She knew she was going to lose consciousness, but she fought it.

"No, please." Her voice sounded so thin she wasn't sure he heard. "I don't know him. I never—"

"Shut up!"

Papa Peter released her, and she slid to the floor. The door opened, and Mama Peter walked in. Through a blur, Asabi noticed she was dressed.

Mama Peter loomed. "What are you doing to her?"

The trace of horror in the woman's voice gave Asabi hope. She heard a crinkling sound and the next thing she knew her wrists were clasped into a cuff.

"She is from Law. I knew it from the first day," Papa Peter said. "Law never came to the house for the devotion. Since she came, he's been here thrice. And she was in his shop yesterday when she told us she lost her way during the charity walk."

"What an evil child. I never suspected."

"Mama, please. It's not true. Please."

Papa Peter pulled Asabi to her feet. "I'm taking her to him. Let him know his scheme has been busted."

"No, Papa." Mama Peter's lips curled inward. "Leave her here. Let him sweat waiting for her."

Asabi heard his sharp laughter. "Then we will need to do more than just cuff her." He threw her on the bed, tied a perfumed handkerchief over her mouth, and then used a rope he must have brought with him to tie her to the bed.

"There. You should think about your life, my dear. Law and Fela and all their evil gang can't beat me in this city."

The door shut with a bang, and Asabi closed her eyes. Her constraints bit into her flesh, causing her pain and discomfort. The handkerchief over her mouth tasted bitter, and the perfume on the handkerchief nauseated her. But what hurt the most was the realization of her plight. She knew, but only now understood why Fela needed to get away. These were not pastors—they were not even good people.

She sobbed and prayed. "Lord, please help me get away from here, if You can."

There was no way of escape. She doubted Davida would look for her. The other woman was evil, too. Asabi had come to the center of the devil's station. What better way could she describe this house? The Peter girls probably didn't know about any of this, and even if they knew, they didn't care. The little boy may not even exist. And the second servant, Mabel, behaved like a ghost, neither seen nor heard.

She rested her head on the soft mattress beneath her, waited, and fell asleep. When she woke, her face was sore from where Papa Peter had struck her. Her mouth was dry, and she had a headache. At least she was conscious. She wasn't sure God had heard her prayer. Amid her pain and anguish, her stomach rumbled. She wished for many things.

The door opened, and she squeezed her eyes shut. A hand jerked her up. She guessed it was Papa Peter. Her eyes flew open. He loomed over her, jaw tight, eyes a harsh squint, not like a man of God at all. He loosened her from the bed but kept the gag and cuffs on. The black clothes he wore made her fear him more. He wouldn't look at her, though she wished he would.

"Your people must be worried by now, so I will be kind enough to take you back to them." He pushed her to the door and on through the house and a back door she'd never seen before. Once outside, he opened the back of a Jeep and flung her inside.

Asabi folded into a ball and took comfort in the fact she'd soon be free of these evil people. She reminded herself of Temly and how she must still be luckier than her friend. More than before, she resolved to return home and prayed God to help her live a good life.

The Jeep pulled up at what Asabi assumed was Law's shop, and Papa Peter got out. For excruciatingly long moments she heard nothing. She pushed herself to a sitting position and glanced through the back window. Outside was dark with patches of light from the neighborhood. Where did Papa Peter go? What did he mean to do with her?

When she thought she would die of waiting, the back door opened, and a handcuffed Law was pushed inside.

Papa Peter snapped. "Let's all go for night vigil."

He got into his Jeep and drove away with them into the night.

Chapter Thirty-Six

Fela dragged his feet through the thicket. His hunger switched to anger, and after walking a few steps, he dropped to his knees and then fell on his back. Too weak to care, he ignored the slight itching of the insect bites on his body, though it had subsided a lot. Law had taught him the secret to healing was to pretend the itch didn't exist for as long as possible.

His conviction now seemed to be a death sentence. There was no way to get out of here. He feared they had walked deeper into the forest rather than closer to home. Perhaps they should have continued along the path set by the animal hooves. The guavas were all eaten, and they hadn't seen anything edible since.

He wondered what grass tasted like.

Temly barely walked now, and when he could, he carried her. All their supplies were gone, and their clothes were dirty and torn.

"Do you hear?"

Temly's whispered question seized his attention. He could hear nothing, but Temly's sensitive hearing was sometimes correct.

His throat was too dry for him to speak. A day had passed without water. He now prayed for the rain he'd once hated. In the past three days, only the delta sun shone day and night. When there was food and water, he'd been grateful, but now he doubted they could last much longer.

"God, if only for Temly's faith, save us or kill us." He rolled onto his side. "I don't hear anything."

She lowered herself beside him. "Remember Hagar. She cried for death, too."

Fela's lips tilted in what should have been a full smile. He closed his eyes. Dear Temly. Now she tried to preach to him when her feet dragged behind her. After what she'd been through, why not? He wondered how beautiful she'd be when she was full-grown. She had a great potential to be attractive with her slim figure and oblong face. Maybe not as pretty or buxom as many of the girls in his school and church back home. He could only imagine. He would never know. They would die here of thirst. Unless it rained today.

His heart struck a new fear. Such a death could be painful and slow. He remembered a movie he heard of about some Irish people who went on a hunger strike to fight something. They started dying after two months. Or was his mind playing tricks on him? Were they Irish or Jews? Was it during the Holocaust?

He preferred to think about Temly being an adult woman. She couldn't compete with any of his old crushes. Those young ladies had all the goods, and he liked them. Women of all ages had gravitated toward him, complimenting his good looks and strong body, but his mentor didn't womanize, and so he didn't. He'd not ever heard Law talk about a date until the last few months when he started contacting someone he met online. He didn't even mention her name. A few dates here and there with harmless pecks on cheeks had been all he cared for.

"I hear a stream."

Fela opened his eyes. He couldn't hear it. Only echoes of the wilderness. Insects, flies, birds if anything at all. Maybe monkeys calling to each other. Since the snake episode, they'd not seen any other wild animal. On several occasions, Fela wished he could hunt but he didn't have the skill or the tools.

"I hear nothing, Temly." Fela swallowed dryness. "Nothing."

She crawled closer and held his hand. He dropped his head to his chest. In his understanding, God always showed up, but where was He now?

Temly squeezed his hand. "I will search."

"No. Let's just wait here. Conserve energy." He sighed. "It should rain tonight."

Temly shifted away from him, but he was too weak to stop her. Maybe it was better she left. He couldn't bear to watch her die anyway. He'd never seen anyone die before he got into this evil forest. Now he prayed for death, too.

He closed his eyes. Let God be true and every man a liar. He couldn't see any future now. Maybe it was better to condition his mind and prepare himself and Temly for eternity. They would never be found. Vultures would devour their flesh before it decomposed. He'd seen them fly low sometimes when they were tired and resting.

He squeezed hot tears from his eyes moments before he heard Temly's weak call.

"Over here, Fela."

The strange pitch in her weak voice got him onto his feet. Water. God always showed up. He knew it.

"Where?" He traced the sound of her voice. He couldn't believe she'd gone so far. "Temly?" He couldn't see her. "Temly?"

He didn't know where the strength in his voice came from. He wished he'd paid attention when she moved away. He searched the surroundings and all he could see was grassy land.

"Temly!" His voice echoed back to him. "Can you hear me?"

"Over here."

He stared around not able to figure out the direction. It sounded from behind him but he didn't think so.

"I can't see you." He moved forward. "Keep talking."

Fela panicked. The forest approached darkness, and with it came night sounds. She needed to keep talking. He couldn't lose her now. And he needed water badly.

He raised his voice as much as he had strength for. "Temly!"

Some creepy animals rushed out of their hiding, and Fela startled. What was the meaning of this, God? Where is she? He was afraid to move. He might go in the wrong direction. The forest changed. He'd seen it happen as they tried to find their way out. He continued to move in one direction, the one he thought should be the right one.

"Temly."

"The stream is here."

But the sound came from another direction, from a distance. He swung around. Was he imagining it? Was he dreaming? He touched his face, and arms, and head.

The last he heard himself question. "Where am I?"

Then everything went black.

Chapter Thirty-Seven

The Jeep must have been on a rough patch for hours.

Asabi's head throbbed from the assault she'd taken, and from her head bumping into the back seat of the Jeep, but she was grateful to be alive. Maybe it would be better to be unconscious — then she'd feel nothing—no pain or fear. Many times when Femi Filips abused her, she'd go blank so there would be no feelings. Now she wished for it. What an irony. No, she didn't desire for such life! She may not want this one, but she didn't yearn for the other one either. Why couldn't she just live a normal life?

Like Temly before she was taken. Like many of the girls in her school. Like Mel who had nothing to worry about but a silly boyfriend.

After Law was thrown into the trunk with her, he'd been quiet. Maybe he was unconscious. He must have hit his head. She tried to talk to him despite her gag, but he didn't reply. Maybe he was gagged, too. What could she do? Why did Papa Peter bring Law into this? Where was he taking them? What did he mean by this night vigil?

Only once did she remember her mother going to church for a night vigil, and it was for prayer. If they were going for such a meeting, they should have arrived. It dawned on her that Papa Peter was probably taking them to the same place he took Fela. The boy had written in his journal he was going with his father, or was she mistaken?

After what seemed like forever across a smooth highway and then a rough road, Asabi fell asleep. She woke up to a slight nudging.

At first, she thought it was the jolting of the vehicle, but then the nudge came again. She remembered she had a co-passenger and grunted.

His voice was low. "Are you okay?"

Papa Peter's voice rose from the driver's seat. "I can hear you clearly. Good, you are talking now."

Asabi went rigid. Law patted her side, perhaps the only part of her body he could reach. She felt his need to communicate but didn't know how.

Law raised his voice. "Peter, yes, I am talking now."

"So, you will be alert when the butchers cut through you. I will make it a special request."

"*Ah*, should be interesting. Will you sell me to ritualists or cannibals?"

Peter laughed. "With a good body like yours, no. Your organs will be harvested while you watch."

Asabi sobbed a moment before she felt the slight nudge again. She closed her eyes beneath the blindfold. Her throat filled with tears, and she couldn't control her cry.

"Finally." Law wheezed. "You take me to where you took Fela, right?"

There was a minute of silence before the abductor's voice came on strong, and a little crack gave away his emotion. Though Asabi wondered if a man like Favor Peter had any conscience at all.

"I told you I'd be rid of you. After you poisoned my son—"

Law laughed. "Fela is not your son. You don't have to pretend with me."

Asabi sucked in her breath. Both at the statement and the sharp pinch of Law's hand on her thigh. What was he trying to do?

He shifted toward her. "Nkiru was a common prostitute. You changed her name. Made everyone call her Mama Peter. All lies. Everyone knew she had an illegitimate child."

"This information will die with you, Lawrence. Because after you're gone, no one will remember you."

"People never forget."

Asabi felt the pinch again. Involuntarily, her handcuffed hands moved toward the area of the pain to rub it and connected with his. He slipped a cold metal object into her hand. Was it a knife?

Papa Peter's voice rang out again. "You have continued to be a thorn in my flesh and my ministry for too long. It ends today."

Law laughed. "It never ends."

She felt the sharp edge. "What?" But it only came out like a moan because of her scented gag.

"I will have the last laugh, Lawrence. You, Fela, and the little clan you built will be destroyed. One by one."

"As long as you hide behind the pulpit and continue your evil, you will never destroy us." Law moved toward Asabi, and his head thumped hers.

He twisted in the dark trunk, and she realized his hands were cuffed in the back. She smoothed her hand over the object. It was a small metal case. Since her hands were cuffed in front, it was easier to hold the case. What would she do with it? Her heartbeat increased. It gave her a great sense of safety and comfort to know someone older and stronger was around to help. But could she trust him? After all, he was a total stranger.

Papa Peter laughed. "The pulpit is a shield, and I have followers who will die for me."

Law blew out air. "You may be rid of me, but God will raise ten more of me to battle you."

"God. Do you know God?"

Law yelled, "Do you?"

Asabi rubbed the case. It was small, like a cardholder. The men continued to exchange harsh words, and the Jeep jiggled from side to side as the terrain grew rougher. She found the opening to the case and slipped it apart. Law wanted her to have it, and she didn't want to risk losing whatever was inside.

Asabi discovered only two needles inside. She frowned. "What is this?" She had to know. Papa Peter was laughing and talking. Asabi moved toward Law. "What—" Her tongue was twisted in her mouth, and her throat had never been so dry. She could cry just because she couldn't communicate with him.

"Give me one," Law whispered.

She understood at once. He would try and pick her lock. She twisted to reach his hand and carefully placed a needle in it.

He moaned. "Hold on."

He held onto her hand and in the most awkward way worked at her cuffs. Meanwhile, he continued to accuse Papa Peter, keeping their quarrel alive. Asabi perked up in the dark. No wonder he had so much influence on Fela and probably other young people around him. He knew how to debate, use words to make one happy or angry.

Asabi sighed when her cuffs were loosed. She pushed off her gag and blindfold and tried to swallow, but it was too painful. "What next?" she whispered.

"Mine."

She had never picked any lock before and couldn't see a thing. The Jeep came to a sudden halt, and Asabi screamed.

Law bellowed, "You'll pay for this, you evil man."

Asabi closed her eyes when the driver's door opened and closed. Papa Peter opened the back. Her nose flared, and her teeth chattered.

Adrenaline pumped through her veins until she thought she'd explode. She tightened her grip on a huge wrench her hand had connected with in a desperate search earlier. She raised it and hit Papa Peter with all her strength. A loud pop, like bone cracking, sounded. Papa Peter dropped like overripe fruit.

The door swung back with force, but Law bridged it with his feet. The wrench dropped from Asabi's trembling hands. She hoped she hadn't killed the man.

"Wonderful," Law said. "Hold it. Hold back the door."

She held the door, and Law wriggled out. "Give me the needle."

Asabi gasped. "It dropped. I'm sorry. The case, too."

Law crouched beside Papa Peter. "No worries. He's out, but not for long. Check inside the car for his mobile phone."

"Okay."

It was too dark to see anything, and the vegetation seemed thick, but Asabi traced the sides of the Jeep to the front. The inner light helped to give illumination, and she found the mobile phone.

She switched on the flashlight and ran back to Law. Within seconds, she found the case and grabbed the second needle. She didn't have time to study her surroundings, though the night sounds of creepy things calling to themselves inferred they were in the middle of a thick forest.

Law told her what to do to pick the lock on the cuffs. When his hands were free, they placed Papa Peter's limp hands in both broken handcuffs and pressed his head down. Then Law pulled down Peter's pants.

Asabi exclaimed. "What are you doing?"

"Diss."

"What?"

"I want to disgrace him." Law pulled off Papa Peter's shirt and rolled it into a ball. "This is what they do to hardened criminals when they catch them. They disgrace them by taking off their clothes." He pulled his shoes off.

Asabi stared into the darkness, afraid of who or what was in the forest. "We need to get out of here. Please."

"We will."

Law found a long chain and created a knot the best he could on the cuffs so the captive would have a hard time freeing himself. Working fast, he cleared out the back of the Jeep of anything able to become a weapon or assist the man's escape. He removed Papa Peter's belt and tied his legs. He also got a handkerchief from his pocket, gagged him, found Asabi's blindfold, and secured it over the man's eyes. Then he closed the trunk.

He threw Papa Peter's clothing and shoes into the backseat and slid into the driver's seat. Asabi rushed in beside him. "I wonder what this place is," he said.

Asabi covered her mouth to hold her tears. "Let's just get away from here."

"Are you all right?"

She could only nod. What if Papa Peter had brought her here alone? What would she have done? How would she have escaped? The reality of what could have been overwhelmed her, and she dissolved into tears.

"It's okay. You're safe now," Law said softly. "Thank God, you're safe."

Asabi sniffed and regained her control. "Thank you so much." She shuddered. "Thank you for—everything."

"I had no choice but to help you." Law stole a glance at her. "It's what a father must do."

Chapter Thirty-Eight

Temly could see the stream several feet away but didn't think her legs would move any more, or rather, her knees. Her palms were sore, and the bruises on her knees stung from all the crawling she'd done. Where was Fela?

"Fela—"

Her voice came out in a mere croak. She just barely heard herself. So how would he hear her, unless he was already coming her way?

She laid her cheeks on the undergrowth. They tickled and pricked, but she couldn't care less. There was no more hope. Death was near. Fela's song rang in her head, the one about Jesus going to Calvary. The road must have been rough and tough. Jesus knew he was going to die, and yet he went. He could have stopped it. He could have manipulated his fate, but he went all the same.

Fela's voice resonated. "Temly!"

She tried to raise her head, but it refused to move. He would have to come closer and find her because she had no more strength in her. Not to move and not to talk. If she didn't get a sip of water soon, she would die. When she'd heard the stream, it had seemed near, but as she moved toward the sound, she realized it was farther. She could see it now, though. So near; so far.

She drifted off to sleep or death. It didn't matter; losing consciousness was most welcome. Her body ached all over. She didn't know what day it was anymore. Last time she ate must have been about a week ago. This didn't matter either.

Angels whirled around her, singing and clapping. She stood and celebrated. They were so beautiful to behold. She saw Fela with them, too, and Asabi. Why would Asabi be here? Was she dead, too? But it didn't matter since everyone was happy. She hugged her friends and laughed. No more pain, no more sorrow, just as Fela told her. She hoped her parents would understand she was in a better place.

But she wasn't. The flapping wings of vultures startled her. She raised her head half an inch, and nearly hit the ugly beak of one seeking a feast. Fear surged adrenaline through her, and she lifted her upper body.

She cried. "Go. Go."

She dragged her body toward the stream. The grass beneath was cool and prickly, but she moved. The vultures moved back but did not leave. Where did they surface? One minute, someone drops dead in the middle of nowhere, and they gather. It's as though the wind carried information to them.

The scavengers gave her unexpected strength, and she lifted herself to her knees. They were bloodied, but if she could get to the stream and drink, she would be able to go back and find Fela. He'd grown even weaker than her in the last few days. Thankfully he'd not faltered till now because she had been so depressed at the start of their awful journey.

Maybe there was a reason for this dreadful experience after all. She had never been a fighter, except for the support she gave Asabi on her abuse. And it had only been verbal and secret. She never faced up to anyone. Back in school, she never stood up to anyone who bullied her, and many had over the years because she was smaller than most of her peers. Until her uncle became the state governor a year earlier, only Asabi had been her friend.

She reached the bank of the stream and pressed her face into the shallow water there. It was just a strip out of nowhere and may have dried up if not for the recent rainfall. It didn't matter. It was water.

She opened her mouth and gulped without restraint. She didn't care if the water was clean or not, whether there were tiny fish or not. This was life. Indeed, she was refreshed right away. She pushed further till she was immersed in it. The coolness soaked her hair to the tip of her toes and she shuddered with relief. Once upon a time, she had detested the rain for getting her wet. Now she thanked God for the touch of cool water on every part of her body.

She laughed and whooped and lifted her hands up. Then she remembered Fela. She had to get back to him before he died of thirst.

She raised herself to her feet, staggered before she gained full control of her feet, and then walked out of the stream and watched the last of the vultures flap a couple of times and take off.

"Good riddance," she mumbled.

Within a minute, she felt a little chill and squeezed the dripping water from the tips of the torn, makeshift robe she wore. Now to find Fela. Where was he? There were trees on every side. How did she come here? It had gotten much darker than when she arrived the stream. Had she slept or fainted so long?

"Fela?" She had to move.

They had never hiked in the dark. She tripped over a stone and fell to her knees. A cry of pain escaped her lips, and some night crawler hurried off at the sound. She took a moment to get her breath. She couldn't see anything. Moving away from the stream could cause her more danger than she dared imagine. She flopped on her bottom and burst into tears she thought she had exhausted.

Chapter Thirty-Nine

A loud knock on his door woke him up, alarmed. The heavy knocking repeated, followed by his father's menacing voice.

"Open this door."

Fela chuckled at the realization. So, Daddy didn't have access for the first time in his thirteen years of existence. He sat up and waited, more amused and curious than furious, which he should be. His friends all thought he was a bad boy because his parents told their parents to steer clear of him. All because he chose to align with someone who showed him care. Law.

The man was alone without a family, and after connecting in the Sunday School class where Law taught pre-teens, Fela found a father figure in him. He'd hoped Law would help him reconcile with his father, but the opposite happened. The few times the two men met and talked, it got ugly, and one day, Pastor Favor Peter made an announcement from the pulpit denouncing Law. The barber was banned from teaching the kids, and a disclaimer was placed on him.

Fela had gone to look for his teacher and mentor after church without his parents' knowledge. Things had taken a downhill turn from there. If his father told him to do something, he ran it by Law before he did it.

He heard a sharp bang and concluded his dad was trying to break down his door. *Nice try*, he thought. The heavy metal bar Law got his carpenter friend to affix to the door while they were all in church could not be broken so easily.

Still, he jumped from his bed and rested against the wall facing the door. He calculated his delight and chose not to laugh till whoever was behind the door left. Law had taught him not to taunt older people, no matter what.

A sharp cut splintered the wood and created a jagged hole in the door. Fela clasped his hand over his mouth but the laughter he tried to curb escaped.

"You bastard. I will deal with you."

His mother's voice came. "Fela, Fela, Fela! Do you want to kill me?"

He felt no sentimentality toward his mother. She was just as mean and uncaring as his father. All they cared about was their image and if they were enriched by the decisions they made. It was part of the reason Law defied them.

He rolled his eyes but said nothing. When he was certain no one remained at his door, he got dressed and unlatched the metal bar. He left the door open. He knew they might come and remove it from the hinge anyway. Nothing they did surprised him anymore.

He stepped out in the corridor, and someone hit him on the back of his head with a big stick before he blacked out. Next thing he knew, he was in a hospital bed and Law was staring into his eyes.

Sharp pain coursed through his body.

****

Fela sat straight. He wasn't asleep and so it wasn't a dream. His palms sweated, and he touched his old wound. The cut had healed well, but the scar was one of the reasons he continued to grow his hair. Fifty stitches had taken care of the damage his father inflicted.

Tears streamed from his eyes. Here he was again, lost in a dangerous forest because Favor Peter refused to care for him. If he got out of this place, he vowed to fight back.

But how? Temly was nowhere in sight. He shuddered and picked himself up.

"Where am I?"

It was already getting dark when he passed out. He ran in all directions against the night, bumping into trees and bushes. "Temly!" His dry throat hurt, and tears burned his eyes. She couldn't survive alone. *Oh dear, where is she?* His weary body cried for rest, but he had to find her. He may not survive to fight his father, but at least he could fight nature to find Temly.

His voice echoed throughout the darkness. "Temly! Where are you?"

Where did she go? He blamed himself for not paying attention, for losing focus.

"God, take me. Kill me but let nothing happen to her." He sobbed. "You brought her to me because she needed help. God, I'm sorry I didn't take care of her when she needed me most."

His knees gave way, and he rolled down a steep hill. Stones and sticks cut across his skin and he gulped for air. A tree stump stopped his fall. He hit his head against the stump and gasped. Sharp pain coursed through him and he wished for oblivion.

He closed his eyes and tried to think through his predicament. The only way he could fight the pain was to block it out. Law had always told him to calm down when he wanted to react. He took several deep breaths, and after a few moments, the pain receded. He grabbed at the bush branches, but his legs refused to carry him.

"Temly."

His cry was only a whisper. She was gone. She might have been a part of his nightmare. He crawled until he gave up. He would die there thinking about her.

He didn't know how long he lay in the dirt. He drifted off and saw Temly clothed in radiant white, laughing at him, and asking him to join her. He reached out to her, but she seemed beyond his reach.

"You're too far," he mumbled.

He opened his eyes and found darkness around him. Then he heard the stream Temly had spoken about. Hope seared his muscles into action. He staggered to his feet and summoned all his strength. The terrain was slippery, and he half-ran, half-slid toward the sound. He reserved the little energy he had left to call her. He knew he'd feel much better after a drink.

The stream seemed farther than he imagined, but the sound grew closer, which encouraged him to keep moving.

Fela did not find the stream. Instead he saw light.

Light.

Where did the light come from? If there was light then there was rescue. Maybe Temly found people at the stream, or had she run into the evil men who wanted to kill them? The thought pushed him ahead.

He stumbled out onto a path just as the brightness came a few meters closer. It became too much for him, and he fell to his knees. He needed to say something, but he also figured whoever held the light must have seen him fall.

He slumped further and hit the ground face first. Could he be helped? Would the bearer of the light help? Or was he dreaming again?

Chapter Forty

Law wasn't as slow or careful as Papa Peter and the Jeep waggled, throwing Asabi in and out of her seat several times despite the seat belt.

"Do you have children?" She remembered Papa Peter's argument and accusations that showed both men had known each other for a long time.

"I have a daughter."

Law's voice seemed like a long distance away. He wore a frown, perhaps because they had broken out of the deep forest and were now on a narrow unpaved road. And to Asabi's surprise, the sun was setting. Where were they? What time was it? She checked the dashboard, six o'clock.

Law didn't seem like someone who wanted to talk about his family. It only piqued Asabi's interest more. If he had a daughter then she understood a little of his compassion.

"Your wife must be worried by now." She raised Papa Peter's phone to his line of vision. "Maybe we can call to let her know you're fine."

Law chuckled. "I don't have a wife. She left me over ten years ago. Eloped with a rich man. She took my daughter with her."

"*Oh*, I'm so sorry."

No wonder he seemed like a sad person. What he must have suffered.

"You never remarried?"

"No." He swallowed. "I loved her, but she wanted more. Always wanted more."

Asabi shrugged. "I think a woman should be happy if her husband loves her. More can always come later."

Law spoke in a quiet voice. "You've grown to become a beautiful woman, Asabi. You look so much like your mother, but you have a good heart."

Asabi experienced a flash of white heat on her face. "You know—my mother?"

"She was my wife."

Asabi gagged. Coupled with the roughness of the road, Law was going too fast or she'd have jumped out of the Jeep. She trembled from head to toe. Who was this man? What was he talking about? Was this the father she'd been in touch with on social media, or was he trying to spook her?

"You—she?"

"Yes, dear. The moment I saw you in the company of the Peters, I knew. I did everything because I wanted to save you from them."

Tears gathered in Asabi's throat. "I don't understand. If you're my father, you're supposed to live in Lagos."

"You said you were in Ibadan, but you could come to Lagos to meet me. I didn't want to complicate matters. That's why I asked us to meet in a restaurant."

"How can you be my father? How did—?"

"I am, Asabi. I married Eni, your mother. I loved you so much. Your mom wanted me to do businesses to bring in more money, give us a better life, but they were illegal, and I refused." He paused. "She started seeing a rich man in town. One day, she packed everything from the house and left a note saying she wouldn't be back." He sighed. "I lost touch with her when she broke off with the man and left town."

Asabi snickered. "I'm not surprised."

"I had no clue where she went. I searched everywhere, sent out notices. I wanted her to return you at least." He slowed down. "Did you have a good life?"

The question was more than Asabi could take. She bent over and gasped for air. Did she have a good life? Who could she blame? She wanted to lash out at this man who was her father. How could he drop this on her? Why didn't he continue searching? Why had he given up on her?

She raised her head. "You look different from what you put online. You don't have dreadlocks in your picture."

"I used an old picture because I didn't want to scare you. I went online because I felt it would increase my chances of finding your mother."

Anger rose like acid in her belly. "Me or my mother? She left you, yet still you yearned for her!"

"Because she could lead me to you, dear."

"You're lying! Let me out of here! You're not my father."

Her anger overpowered her, and she grabbed the steering wheel. Law swerved off the road and then back. He seized her arm.

He was lucky to see a staggering figure tear through the bushes along the road just in time before he hit him. The person had tattered clothes dangling from his shoulders, and he raised his hands above his head before he fell to his knees.

Law panted. "Fela?"

Chapter Forty-One

"Fela!"

Fela felt a cool touch to the back of his head. A smaller light shone on his face and sent rockets of pain through his eyes. He wished he could tell them to take it away. Where was he? Who was this?

The hand opened one eye and then the other.

"We need to get him to the hospital."

The voice was familiar. No, they couldn't take him away. He needed to find Temly first. They held him by the waist and heaved him up, but Fela struggled. He couldn't leave with this person without Temly.

"No. Please." He opened his mouth to take more air. "My. Sister. She's in—inside."

"Fela, look at me. It's Law."

He opened his eyes and tried to focus, but pain accosted his face. He must have some injury to hurt like this. "Water."

"There's a bottle in the door of the driver's side."

Fela heard footsteps. There were two of them. A moment later, the bliss of water down his parched throat sent shudders through his body. He gripped the hand on the bottle and then remembered Temly would need water, too.

He released his grip. "My sister—"

"Fela, it's me. Law. Look at me."

"Law." Was he back home? "Where am I?"

"We don't know, but the most important thing is you are alive. And we need to get you out of here."

Fela felt the gentle lift of the upper part of his body. "No. I can't leave."

"You have to. It's evening. It's late, and I don't know where we are. We need to get as far away from here as possible. And we need to do it, now."

Fela struggled against the hold. "I can't leave her." He lurched backward and fell.

"Who? What sister?"

"My sister." Fela focused. "Law."

This was his friend. The water had refreshed him, and he could comprehend. By some mighty power, Law was here in the forest, and he had a car with him and water. What more did they need to search for Temly?

Law pulled him back. "I don't know who you're talking about, but we have to leave now."

Fela snatched his hand from the grip with energy he didn't know he possessed. "Leave. But I have to find her."

"I'm not letting you go back into the forest. Your sisters are at home, so I don't even know what you're talking about—"

They heard a rumbling sound like approaching thunder.

"Rain is coming."

For a moment, Fela thought it was Temly. The voice sounded small, just the way she sounded when she was worried, but the girl with Law wasn't Temly.

"We'll leave now." The thunderous sound came again, and Law glared toward the Jeep. "I don't think it is rain."

Fela stared at the pretty girl. She seemed so frightened. Had Law come to rescue her? "Who's she?"

"My daughter."

Fela never knew he had a daughter. It brought urgent questions to his mind. What was Law doing here?

"Please help me, Law. I can't leave her here."

"You don't know what you are saying. Maybe being in the forest for so long has twisted your mind." Law reached out to him again.

He drew back. "What are you doing here, anyway? Where is this?"

"I don't know. It's a long story and—"

Anyone who heard would think he was crazy. "I'm going to find my sister."

"What nonsense sister?"

The rumbling lasted a little longer, and the girl with Law glanced at the Jeep. Fela followed her gaze. Why was she so nervous?

"I think he has regained consciousness."

Law ordered Fela. "Get in the car."

"Help me."

"No. Get in, and let's go. We can come back for her. You need medical help."

Fela didn't care. He must have a concussion because the pain in his head refused to go away. Yet, he would never forgive himself if by any chance no one returned to find Temly.

He took several steps back. "I can't leave her."

Law sighed. "I'm going to regret this."

A deep groan emanated from the back of the Jeep followed by sounds of scuffle. The three of them spun toward the sound.

"Asabi, come."

"We can't leave him."

"I can't carry him, can I? Should I haul him into the Jeep?"

"You can. How can you leave him?"

Law opened the back door and brought out Papa Peter's confiscated clothes. "At least put some clothes on."

Fela took the clothes with shaky hands. "Where did you get these from? Daddy's clothes."

Law exhaled. "I can't stand here and tell you tales by moonlight, can I?" He got into the driver's seat.

"I can't wear his clothes."

Asabi stood for several moments before rushing back into the Jeep. Law revved the engine, raising enough dust to serve Fela a meal, and drove forward at a ridiculous speed.

Fela watched him go. He clutched the fresh clothes to him, nauseated by his father's scent, yet comforted by the feel of warmth and safety. How did Law get here and know he would need clothes? He thought of the rags Temly had on, too.

"I can't leave Temly," he whispered. He couldn't wear Favor Peter's clothes either.

The Jeep came to an abrupt halt; at the same speed, it reversed and Law put his face in Fela's. "Where is she?"

Fela closed his eyes.

"Inside. Let's go find Temly!"

Chapter Forty-Two

Unknown location, Nigeria Unknown day, unknown time

"Temly!"

Finding Fela meant they would find Temly. How could this be? Asabi didn't know but thanked God for guiding her here. She was exhausted from all the things happening at once and didn't comment. They walked through the bushes Fela had come from, calling to Temly.

Thoughts of Law being her father seemed so farfetched she had to push them aside to contemplate later. How could it be true?

Law stopped and called to Fela and her. "I think the best thing is to go back and get help. Roaming in the dark puts all of us in danger."

Fela groaned. "No. I can't leave her in this place. I lost her days ago. I can't—"

Asabi's voice was hollow. "How many days?" She'd been through hell and back, but to be lost in this thick dwarfed anything she had ever suffered in her life.

"It doesn't matter. Fela, be reasonable. We don't know the danger we face here. And Temly could be anywhere. Besides, Asabi is terrified."

Fela faced Law. "Then go home with her—"

Asabi gasped. "I want to find Temly," she rushed to say, "and what terrifies me is she's somewhere in this bush. Alone."

"But the battery of this cell phone is running down, and we will all be back to square one," Law said. "And it's better to search in daylight with more people than—"

"So go, Law. You can come back for Temly and me."

"Do you hear yourself? You're weak. You'll get lost. And I don't even know where this is. Perhaps the GPS may work at some point, but there haven't been any signals for a whole day, driving round and round this forest. We can only follow the road and hope it leads us somewhere. If the fuel doesn't run out first."

"Exactly. I agree with you. But I am not leaving this place till I find Temly. How is it so difficult for you to understand?"

Law yelled, "Don't be rude, Fela. When did you become more concerned for anyone but yourself?"

"*Oh*, see who's talking. Who taught me to be me? Who—"

"Why don't we pray?" Asabi didn't recognize her own voice. The other two paused midway through their argument. Once she requested prayer, her confidence grew. "I know I've not been a good Christian before now, but I think we should pray, and God will answer us." She licked her lips. "I can't leave Temly here, either." She bit down on her trembling lip. "I'm the reason she's in this horrible place, and I can't go anywhere until we find her." They glared at her. "Please, let's just pray. God will show us where she is."

Fela summed up Law's reluctant profile. "I agree."

Law sighed. "Let's be realistic."

Asabi went on her knees. "God brought me here. I know now it was God, not me or my mind. He guided me to Warri where I found out about Fela."

Fela joined her on his knees. "I never believed in God. My parents put me off Him with their ways. You taught me Sunday School and built my faith but drew me back the moment you fell from the faith. But now I know God is real." He lifted his hand to Law. "You once believed, too."

Law knelt and held out his hands to Fela and Asabi. "You children make me look silly when you talk so."

Fela cleared his throat. "As the only person with a good religious background and upbringing, permit me to say the prayers."

His attempt at humor was not lost on the others. He raised his voice and sang the song in his spirit through his wilderness experience. Strength entered their voices, and from one song to the other, the three raised an altar of worship to God.

Asabi half-expected a miracle but nothing happened. When Fela rounded up his prayer, they all sat on the ground in the darkness.

"The battery is out," Asabi whispered.

Law's gruff voice cut through the still night. "This silence is creepy."

Fela sniffed. "We got used to it."

They all fell silent again.

Asabi's stomach groaned, and Fela chuckled. "What do we do now?"

"I could charge the phone in the car but it might take quite a while," Law said. "And the battery of the Jeep may run down."

"You think God heard our prayer?" Asabi said.

"I think He did." Law reached out to her in the dark and squeezed her hand. "I found you. It means God hears prayers."

"Yeah, I was going to ask you," Fela said.

Law spoke softly. "It's a long story for another day, Fela."

"Well, I'm alive. It means God is real." Fela shifted. "*Ah*, I miss my bed. *Hmm*. How long ago did you say I disappeared from home?"

Law's voice thickened. "Almost two weeks."

Fela gasped. "Totally insane."

"Temly disappeared about ten days ago, too," Asabi said. "Everything has changed since then. It's as if the life we lived before never existed."

"It's the way God works sometimes," Law said. "Everything will be fine when Fela gets back home to face his dad." He sighed. "Your dad is in the Jeep, by the way. We're holding him hostage."

Fela did not respond and Law moved toward him. "Fela?" He touched him. "He's asleep."

Asabi moaned. "What a poor soul. What he must have gone through in this horrible place."

"I remember the day your mother left me," Law said softly. "I thought my life had ended." He paused. "She took everything in the house. She took all my barbering instruments because we had only two rooms. I used one room for my shop, and we lived in the other."

Though she couldn't see him well, she heard the pain in his voice.

"I'd gone to the market. By the time I returned, the house was empty. She left a note saying I shouldn't look for her because she would never come back."

Asabi snickered. "She's married to someone else."

"I know from her profile. Femi Filips, the millionaire pharmacist."

And child molester, Asabi wanted to say but refrained. She didn't know him well enough, and this wasn't the time or place. One day, maybe.

Asabi slid to the ground, weeds and thorns, and stones scratched her skin, but she was too exhausted to care. She still couldn't believe she was here. With her father, a barber.

Chapter Forty-Three

Dawn broke on the three of them sprawled across a grassy plain.

Fela wakened, but he was too weak to do much else than watch Law, who sprang to his feet and surveyed the surroundings. He could only thank God for giving him this new day.

Law walked a small perimeter of the area, amidst short trees and tall grasses, doubtless looking for Temly. Fela sat up. How could he have slept without finding her? His body ached, but he pushed the pain away and summoned all his strength.

"Good morning," he called out. "I'm sorry I slept in." He felt a little irritated Law let him sleep so long. Wouldn't his mentor think he didn't care much about Temly?

Law arched his eyebrow toward him. "No need to apologize. We all needed sleep."

Fela sized up the girl rolled into a ball. Law's daughter? Interesting. He'd never talked about a family anywhere. He'd not seen her well the previous night, and now curled up, she seemed so vulnerable. Beautiful though. She must have her mother's light color because Law was dark-skinned.

Fela heaved himself to his feet. "I have to find Temly." The pain refused to let up.

"We will." Law walked back. "I was trying to see if we could get a trail the Jeep could drive through. It's a four-wheel."

Fela scowled. "Did I hear you say my dad was somewhere or was I dreaming?"

Law nodded. "He's in the Jeep. We held him. I'm sorry, Fela. There was no—"

"We don't have time." Fela tapped Asabi. "We need to look for Temly."

Law nodded. "Yes."

Asabi stretched. "Good morning."

"Good morning, Asabi. I hope the night wasn't too bad," Law said.

She yawned. "We're still alive."

"I pray Temly is, too." Fela rocked back and forth. "Do you know how we got here?"

Law gave a curt nod. "Yes. At least the general direction we came from." He heaved a heavy sigh. "I wish I could do this alone. You two look so weak."

"I'm not too weak to find Temly." Fela squared his shoulders. "Let's go, please."

They walked in one direction, sometimes apart but not too far to lose sight of one another, calling her name. The sun rose and scorched the team, but they continued.

The plain grassland condensed as they went, and Law called for them to stop. "I think I should charge the phone in the Jeep and call for help, if I can get a signal."

Fela grimaced. He'd learned in the past week the weather changed without warning, and the landscape could turn hostile fast. "Do you know where we are?"

"I have a rough idea. I'm good with landmarks and loca—"

"Listen!" Asabi gripped Law's hand. "Temly! Can you hear her?" she screeched. "Temly."

Before they could stop her, she ran east through the tall grass. The two men ran after her. Fela couldn't hear anything, but he wouldn't give up. He blamed himself for letting Temly trail off. If his hearing had served him, they'd have been together through the rough night. They'd have found the stream together and gotten rescued by Law.

She was in a crawling position less than twenty meters from where they'd stopped searching the previous night, badly bruised and much of the red cloth tied around her torn. Power surged into Fela's bones, and he outran Asabi to reach Temly first. He fell on his knees before her and hugged her to him. Hot tears ran down his cheeks.

"My Temly. My Temly."

"Fela," she said weakly. "Thank God."

Fela pressed a kiss on her forehead and sobbed. Relief and pain soared through him. It was over. She'd been found. Alive.

Asabi dropped to her knees beside him, and soon Law joined them.

Fela tried to lift Temly but fell back on one knee.

"Here." Law took her from his arms and rose. "She's soaked. We need to get back to the Jeep." He waited for the vulnerable teens to look at him. "You two just follow me. I know exactly where we are."

He led them back the way they had come.

The Jeep wasn't as far away as Fela had thought. He marvelled at how close he had been to Temly yet didn't hear her or the stream. He gawked at the strip of water again. It could have saved their lives. It wasn't far from where they'd found Temly. But then, if he'd found the stream with Temly, he probably would not have found Law.

It was over.

Nothing else was important now. They'd been found. Over a week of horror had come to an end. Fela didn't have any answers, but he planned to find them, especially since his father had deserted him.

His priorities had changed, and thoughts about Favor Peter weighed on his heart. What next? He had to expose his occult activities. But how? And what would the consequences be? His father was a national figure. Wouldn't it be better to keep it quiet? Did his mother know? It was hard to tell. Where would he live? Because he knew he'd never be able to return home.

Fela fought to push the thoughts away and focus on the joys of being alive, but it was difficult.

A few meters from the rough road, Law stopped. They had a clear view of the Jeep, but something didn't seem right.

Asabi exclaimed. "The back door is open."

Whoever was on the road could see them, too.

"We need to approach carefully," Fela said.

"No." Law gestured with his head. "Let me go alone."

"Of course not!" Fela said. "If anyone is there, they've seen us already."

"Besides, we're too tired to run." Asabi glanced at her best friend. "And I doubt Temly can even stand."

Fela reached out. "Let me carry her. If there is a fight, at least you can defend us, Law."

Law hesitated. "I can't risk your lives."

Asabi shook her head. "We'll be fine. We can fight, too." She raised her eyebrows at Fela, and he nodded.

Law placed Temly in Fela's arms. He staggered a bit but soon got his bearing. The ache in his head soared, and for a moment he felt he would fall, but he took a deep breath and closed his eyes against the dizziness.

"Stay behind me," Law said.

They approached with caution. When they reached the road, Fela and Asabi stopped, and Law moved to the Jeep. He walked around and called out to the teens.

"He's gone. There's no one here."

Asabi took a deep breath. "Come, let's leave this place."

Law opened the door and helped Fela lay Temly down. He climbed into the driver's seat, and Asabi sat beside him. Fela got in behind and cradled Temly's head.

Law launched the Jeep onto the road. "Let's just pray this road leads to somewhere safe. I think you three need medical attention."

Temly moaned. "I heard your prayer last night. I slipped and fell at the stream and hit my head—"

Fela smoothed back her rough hair. "*Shh.*"

"I couldn't call anymore. Then I heard you singing and praying and tried to crawl out." Temly closed her eyes. "I'm so glad you prayed last night."

Chapter Forty-Four

The man drove like demons were in hot pursuit.

Temly didn't care about who he was or how Fela knew him. The most important thing to her was they had been found. Fela was her hero, and nothing would ever change this. When she had realized she was alone again, she'd been terrified. She wouldn't have survived without her hero.

He smoothed her hair from her face, and she relished his every touch. She didn't want to be anywhere else but here. Maybe the whole kidnapping thing happened for a reason. To bring them together.

Her mind raced to Asabi. How did Asabi get here? So many questions, no answers. Her stomach rumbled with hunger, and her head and backside ached. She knew for sure she had injured her left ankle. She was thirsty, too.

The Jeep seemed to hit every pothole, and the road had more holes than level ground. She closed her eyes, hoping some of the pain would go away, but it didn't.

She nudged Fela and got his attention. "You're cute," she whispered.

He laughed and traced his finger over her cheek. "You think so? With the way I must look?"

Temly gave a mock bow. "Yes."

Law peeked through the rear-view mirror. "What's the joke?"

"I'm not sure you'll understand." Fela winked at Temly. She giggled, but the pain at the side of her face cut it short.

"Try me."

"Well—"

Temly gasped. "Don't say it."

"I have a young lady here hitting on me," Fela said.

"*Haha*! I can't believe—"

"What exactly is so funny?" Asabi's voice quavered. "We're in the middle of nowhere. There's a dangerous man on the loose, and we don't even know where we're going or where we are, and you two are joking?"

Temly and Fela exchanged looks. Everyone understood their predicament, and she felt guilty, though she didn't see why she couldn't try to make light of their situation by being funny. Fela was indeed cute, and she'd earned the right to feel free at last.

"I'm sorry. But I'm not sure you've been where we were in the past week," Fela said. "Besides, we didn't invite you into this."

"It's okay, Fela," Law said. "Asabi has been through a lot, too. It's natural for her nerves to be on edge."

"Only her nerves are on edge. At least she's had food and water and a warm bed."

Temly pushed to a sitting position. "Fela, please."

Asabi raised her voice. "You don't know me, so don't judge me."

Fela matched her volume. "Then don't judge me either."

"Stop it, both of you." Law glanced sideways. "We should all be grateful we're alive." He stole a look backward. "We're not in this forest because we got some divine direction to find you. We were beaten and cuffed and brought here for heaven knows what purpose." He paused. "By your father, Fela. Now he's missing, disappeared by his evil powers even though we left him cuffed in the back. Do you know what this could mean? We have too much at stake right now. We can't fight among ourselves."

Temly thought of what this meant. Where did Fela's father go? How did he leave if he was tied?

Fela grumbled. "I'm not fighting anybody."

"It's okay, Fela. Asabi, you, too, please. I just want to get home," Temly said softly.

Fela drew her head back to his lap. "I'm sorry."

She tapped his arm. "Let me sit up a little."

"Are you sure?" Fela touched her temple. "There's a lump here."

"It hurts!" She withdrew his hand. "But the potholes—"

"We're nearing a village," Law said. "Let's see if we can get the name."

No one responded, but Temly noticed Asabi's back straightened and she became more aware of the surroundings. Fela also sat up. The road improved a little and became wider as the vegetation changed to rows of tall trees. Law slowed and scanned the road left and right. There were areas of farmland and huts on both sides of the road. Temly's head pounded, and she dropped it to her chest.

Fela patted his chest. "Rest your head here at least." She took his invitation with a soft smile.

Clusters of huts gave way to mud and blockhouses with some of the farmers presenting farm products on the roadside. Some bush animals, both fresh and roasted, were also on display.

Law pointed at one of the roadside hawkers. "It looks like cars use this route a bit."

"We should soon find the name of the town," Fela said and continued to look outside.

A little while later, they entered the town.

"We're in Ikire," Law said. "I saw a sign."

Fela let out a loud breath. "I don't know it."

"It's close to Ibadan," Law said. "Asabi, you should know about it."

Asabi shrugged, still begrudged. "Only heard the name."

"Seems the forest road leads into a main town. We need to find a hospital first." He signaled toward Papa Peter's cell phone where it had been plugged in to charge. "And we can call your parents, Temly."

Those were the best words she'd heard in her entire life.

Chapter Forty-Five

They found a clinic, and Law drove into the small parking space.

Fela insisted on carrying Temly, though he knew he was as weak as she was. Asabi felt jolts of jealousy because of Fela's attentions on Temly yet hated the feeling. No matter what she had been through, both had been through worse, and she had to come to terms with it.

She had no reason to be angry with him, but she was. On the contrary, she had every right to fret over their predicament. His evil father had escaped. She believed he had help, so if he did, what could he be up to?

They walked into a small, dirty reception area with litter on the floor and the walls grungy with a need to be repainted. The stench of filthy bathrooms wafted in at intervals.

A young woman dressed in mufti greeted them from behind a short counter, though her open horror at the appearances of the newcomers was evident in her dropping jaw and widening eyes. Law answered her surprised questions while Fela found a bench and sat with Temly in his arms. Asabi swallowed her discontent. She couldn't believe Temly didn't seem glad to see her. She hadn't said a word to her but rather gave all her attention to Fela. What had she possibly gone through with this young man? Asabi stood listless while the clinic's strong smell of stench and antibiotics caused her nausea.

"I have three teenagers who are traumatized. Is there a doctor on duty to examine them?" Law spoke the local language.

"What sort of trauma?"

The woman couldn't be more than twenty years old. She arched her neck, glared at the three of them and swallowed hard.

"They were beaten." Law waved at Fela. "The other one fell, and she can't walk."

The lady squeezed her nose. "Beaten by whom?"

Law pursed his lips. "Assailants."

She narrowed her eyes. "Did you go to the police?"

"No, we came here first."

"You have to report at the police station. First." She walked to a row of small plastic baskets hung on the wall and took out three tattered forms. "You have to register. Five thousand naira per person. First."

Law crossed his arms. "Which first?"

She shoved the forms at him. It was just too expensive for such a dirty clinic.

"Okay." Law sighed. "But we don't have money here, and these kids need attention. We were on a journey and—"

"You have to pay or go somewhere else."

"Please listen. We were attacked on the road. Once these children see the doctor, I'll look for money to—"

The receptionist took the forms from his limp hand and returned them to the basket. "Sir, unless they register, they cannot see anybody." She folded her arms and glared at the space behind him and the teenagers.

Law considered Fela and Asabi and scratched the back of his neck. Temly slept in Fela's arms, so pale and thin.

"We need to register to have you see a doctor."

"Ibadan is not far from here. Let's just go," Asabi said.

"Good idea." He licked his lips. "I'm sure Temly's family will gladly loan us money for food and fuel, then we can get back to Warri."

Fela gaped. "I'm not—"

Asabi shook her head. "I'm staying—"

Asabi spoke first. "I'm not staying in Ibadan. I'm going back to Warri with you."

Law's eyes darkened. "I don't think your mother will—"

"I don't care what my mother says or does."

Law gasped. "Asabi—"

Fela swallowed. "I'm staying in Ibadan till I'm sure Temly is okay."

Of all the things he'd said, Asabi found this the most irritating. "Her family will take good care of her, so they don't need you."

Fela dismissed her with a frown. Who was he to look at her with disrespect? She pursed her lips.

"I think we should be on our way," Law said. "When Temly wakes, it will be good to have her in safe hands. We can iron out the details of what to do next on the way."

They headed for the door, and the receptionist murmured some words. Law waved the kids to go on but spoke to her.

"Did you say something?"

The lady scoffed. "Please go. Armed robber."

Law shook his head and joined the others at the door. "Frustrating," he muttered under his breath.

Asabi didn't know the way out of Ikire, but Law did. He maneuvered onto the highway. After they were all settled back into the journey, he said, "I think you should see your mother at least before—"

"Don't you want me anymore? I thought you were ready to take me as your daughter." Asabi wanted to scream or cry. She didn't know what she felt anymore.

Law lowered his voice. "Don't talk like this, Asabi. I was only trying to help."

"Help how? Don't bother. I can take care of myself," she said. "After all, you didn't know or care about where I was. And you lied you were in Lagos all along."

She wished she could be in a better mood but seeing Fela so stricken with Temly rankled her. She hated men, but when she saw Fela's picture, a certain attraction for him was triggered. He didn't strike her as gay at all, not then and not now. Davida must have been wrong, and she wanted to believe the best about her father.

All worn out and ragged seemed to increase Fela's appeal, but he was cranky and overwhelmed by Temly. Where did he think he'd stay in Ibadan? Asabi could almost vouch Temly's family would not accept him, especially when they heard about his evil background. It gave her some comfort. He'd be forced to return to Warri, maybe not to his family. She had a vision of her living in the same house with him and Law. It made sense.

Temly, her once-upon-a-time best friend, did not feature in this picture. She'd be with her rich and happy family, attend her prestigious academy for girls, deal with silly girls like Mel, be a local celebrity, and forget she ever existed. Cool, too. She had a few questions for Temly as well, but for now they'd have to wait.

Her most pressing need was to find somewhere to live if Lawrence the barber refused to take her in.

****

After several awkward minutes of silence, Law brought up the options available to them going forward. Fela insisted he wasn't leaving till he was sure he could come back to Temly, and Asabi maintained she wasn't staying in Ibadan. Temly slept on.

Whatever Asabi had against her mother must be huge, and Fela hoped Law would tell him about it when this was over. Not as though he cared to know. Unlike Temly, Asabi was stunning at first sight. Despite their tough circumstances, she remained beautiful. Her eyes had a spark, and her lips were well shaped. Not that it mattered to him. Temly was his princess. But he wondered how sweet Temly could have been this saucy girl's best friend less than two weeks ago.

The first few minutes after they left the clinic at Ikire, Law and Asabi had torn at each other with words Fela found shockingly personal. He wondered what their story was and couldn't wait to be told.

Law tapped Asabi. "Money is the main issue for us, and you think it won't be offensive if we asked Temly's father to give it? I think the honorable thing to do is to ask for a loan." He sighed. "Temly will be cared for by her family, but we can't heap our welfare on them."

Asabi mumbled a response Fela couldn't understand, and he closed his eyes. Money was a problem all right. He'd lost everything in his forest experience. There was no way he could go back home now. For his father to have disappeared meant the man was still deep in his evil practices. Some evil powers enabled a magician's disappearance act, and he would not be surprised his father had it. But God had brought them this far. He could take care of the future. Anything more was worry, and it would do nothing to add to the help he needed.

Law's voice droned on, and Fela drifted off to sleep. He woke up with a start when the Jeep came to a halt, and Law switched off the engine.

"We're here."

Chapter Forty-Six

Several cars were parked inside the Coles' compound.

Fela clenched his jaw in anticipation and trepidation. The questions in his mind were enormous, but he would not, could not, leave Temly. He would marry her. He'd come to the conclusion long ago when he thought they both would not survive the forest. If God saved them the way He did, then nothing could stop him from loving her forever.

Asabi's sneers and snickers each time he fussed over Temly infuriated him. If she was Temly's best friend, he guessed he'd have to deal with her for as long. Something else bothered him. Was his princess' family also this different from her? He had to be prepared to face them as well, whatever the case. He believed Temly's people loved her, who wouldn't? She was such an adorable person, and she wore her heart in her eyes.

He gazed at the object of his adoration. She was still fast asleep. Good. He took deep breaths as Law found a parking space beside a vehicle marked "police." Great. At least they would be safe here. Thoughts of his father rose like acid in his throat, but he forced them down. Not now. Temly was most important.

Law sighed. "Here at last." He twisted around so he could see Temly.

Fela sniffed. "She's still asleep."

"I guess you should wake her," Asabi said. "And let her know she's home before people start screaming and the excitement—"

Fela swallowed. Asabi's words just seemed to come out wrong. Couldn't she just sound—nice? He shook his head. "No. She doesn't like being woken up."

"Asabi is right, Fela."

"I'd rather you both go inside first and let her parents know she's here." Fela cracked his knuckles. "She's weak, tired, and dirty. She hasn't had anything to eat or drink in at least two days." His voice thickened with emotion. "I don't want to wake her just yet. She needs better care."

Law nodded. "You're both right." He touched Asabi's hand. "Do you agree with Fela?"

Asabi shrugged and got out of the Jeep. She stretched, a sign of how tired she was, too, but Fela couldn't find much sympathy for her.

He beckoned to Law. "Why is she acting so ugly?"

"She's been through some unpleasant things, Fela. And she came to Warri on her own to find Temly. Try be a little nicer, please."

A loud scream rent the air, and they both glanced toward the direction of the sound, which came from somewhere inside Temly's home — a beautiful duplex. Temly startled awake and gripped Fela's chest.

Fela groaned. "*Huh*, just what I was trying to avoid." He saw a woman run out of the house, with several people behind her. But the woman's focus was on Asabi. Asabi's mother? The resemblance was striking.

Fela put his index finger on his closed lips. "*Shh*. You're alright. You're home."

"I'm home? *My* home?" Temly struggled to a sitting position. But Fela gently held her down.

"Yes." He noticed the woman hugged Asabi's neck. "I don't think they know you are here yet."

She led Asabi back into the house and others followed. Law hung around as though uncertain of his position.

One of the people who'd come outside, a young man Fela concluded would be a member of Temly's family because of the resemblance, glanced in his direction. It was at that same moment Temly rose again. The young man's mouth fell open.

"Temilola?" He gasped and lunged for the car door. "Temly!"

"Please don't raise alarm," Fela said. "She's weak." But he doubted the other man heard.

In a moment, he was shoved aside, and the young man carried Temly like a new bride. Tears streamed down his face as he hugged her to himself in an impossible angle at the back seat of the Jeep. If given a choice, Fela would have stepped out and avoided being crushed in the triangle.

Temly said weakly, "Tayo." She blinked at Fela. "My brother."

Chapter Forty-Seven

It wasn't possible to sneak Temly into the house as Fela had suggested. Her family loved her too much, and it soon became evident.

Asabi knew once someone saw them the whole house would erupt, and that's just what happened. Her mother had sighted them first. What was *she* doing at the Coles'? Asabi had vowed she'd never go back to her. To think the woman left her father for another man was unbearable, and then that she'd married a pedophile and watched him violate her all these years? Yet, in all the ensuing fanfare, those facts were trivial.

A circus of events took over. Temly's parents and brothers wept, laughed, hugged her, stood back, and only glared at her. Since she left, Asabi discovered there had been tighter security measures in the house. She noticed cameras had been installed, and the police car outside wasn't for visitors. The Coles now had police protection round the clock.

A doctor arrived within the hour to tend to Temly and Fela. Mrs. Cole made several calls to her friends and family, drinks were brought in, and music played from a sound system. Governor Tai Cole drove to the house amidst pomp and held a press conference. A weak Temly stood in front of cameras for just a few seconds before the doctor insisted she needed to be back in bed. Fela stuck to her like chewing gum, despite the family's thronging.

Tunji tried to stop Fela from going into Temly's room, but she argued in his favor, and he obliged her.

Law stood in the crowd with his dirty and torn shirt and his hair in tangled locks, an awkward sight to behold. Asabi watched her mother's reaction to him. There was none. Eni Filips pretended Law was not in the room, and this aggravated her even more. Such insolence. Instead, Eni stayed close to Temly's mother like they were besties or something. It sickened Asabi to her stomach.

Thanks to Mrs. Cole, they all bathed in the guest bathroom and ate chicken pepper soup with boiled white rice and vegetables. Fela shampooed his cornrows and brushed it till most of the loose tangles along the rows had smoothened out. Mrs. Cole offered her guest room to Law, so he could rest before discussing the future. The governor demanded full details of what happened to help with the other investigations, and in Asabi's mind, pursued his political career. Everything ended up partisan.

After the brief press conference, Asabi walked into Temly's room to get some sleep and talk to her friend but more to escape her mother. She hadn't seen the deplorable Femi Filips, but she was sure he would show up before the day ended. The man liked cheap publicity.

Temly lay cuddled on the bed while Fela lounged on a couch that had been moved into the room for him. Did he think he'd sleep in Temly's room?

He stood when she entered. "Do you know where Law is? I need to talk to him."

Good, Asabi thought. "Law is in the guest room," she said. "I think it will be good for you to get some rest as well. Temly is fine, as you can see."

She couldn't believe he could look any better considering the ordeal he just passed through, but he did since he took a bath, put on a pair of jeans and t-shirt from Tayo's wardrobe, and didn't seem angry anymore. He even jested with her, and what a nice smile on a guy.

He nodded. "Thanks. I think I will." He walked to the bed and caressed Temly's face. "I'm close by if you need me."

Temly made a comic face. He pressed his lips to her forehead and walked out. Asabi took deep breaths. What could she say to her bestie? They seemed so different now. Did they ever have anything in common? She felt different and could sense a change in Temly, too.

"*Wow,* Asabi. You look like an old woman," Temly said, breaking the ice. Both girls laughed.

She sat beside Temly and touched the same cheek Fela just did. "Temly, what happened to us?" Tears gathered in her eyes. "I'm so glad, you're back."

Temly shook her head. "I can't believe this all happened. Fela said I should write a book."

Asabi's hand dropped to her side. "You started kissing."

Temly's eyes widened. "No!"

"*Hmm.* What about the one on your forehead? Just now."

"Honestly, I think Fela is just overwhelmed. He's never been this—emotional."

Asabi walked to the other side of the room. "But you like him."

"I do. A lot." Temly shrugged. "But after what we've been through, you would, too."

"I guess."

Temly started to move but winced. "I wish I could shake you. I'm still me."

"You wish."

"I'm still your best friend. Fela is just—" Temly rolled her eyes. "Fela. I don't know why he isn't nice to you, but he'll come round. You'll see."

She smirked. "Anyway, it's all right."

"Asabi—yeah sure. So, tell me what happened to you."

She'd been eager to talk about her experiences. She wanted to know what Temly thought. Her words jumbled out, and when her emotions threatened to overtake her, she paused and then continued.

"You see, Fela's father is such an evil man," Asabi said after she'd told her story. "I thought I had ugly parents but his, *huh*!"

Temly nodded. "Fela told me his father was the one who took him to the forest and left him there."

Asabi gasped. "Are you kidding? What? Poor guy. No wonder he didn't say anything much about him. Papa Peter has this creepy voice, Temly." She lowered her voice and made it hoarse. "Let's go for night vigil."

Temly gasped. "Is this what he says? It's—desecration of something holy! We don't even know what he'll do next."

"Do you know a lot about Fela?"

"I know him like I know you now."

She rolled her eyes. "Do you know he's gay?"

Temly laughed. But seeing Asabi's frown, she clasped her hand over her mouth. "He's so not gay."

"I saw his photos in his house. He wore make-up, and his housekeeper said so, too."

Asabi planned to ask Law, too because she just couldn't imagine living with a father who abused teenagers in any way. The subject must be thrashed out. She knew she ought to have considered this before she asked to stay with him, but her fears made her fluctuate between trusting and not trusting Law.

Temly giggled. "He told me he dressed like a girl to drive his parents crazy."

"Are you sure?"

"I believe him." Temly shrugged. "So, do you want to leave school and start over with your dad? I mean, it's incredible you found him, but—"

"I can't go back to my mom for sure."

"You can stay here, you know."

"I can't live so close to her now, Temly. It's so complicated."

Chapter Forty-Eight

A priest came to the Coles' house to hold a service and serve communion. Law stood with Fela at the back of the large sitting room while several state dignitaries, including Temly's uncle, Governor Tai Cole, paraded the two girls in front of journalists, so many they could fill a hall.

Overnight, tents had been erected outside the compound, and a catering outfit attended to guests round the clock. Security details tripled because the governor, commissioner of police, and several other state officials were present.

Asabi was on display as a heroine who'd done the impossible to go and look for her friend.

"She said she wasn't coming back till she found her friend!" The governor had ranted in his speech the day before.

Now the two girls knelt in front of the mantle place and received communion.

"Not sure the priest likes this crammed room for such an elaborate razzle-dazzle. He'd have preferred this was done at the stadium." Law sighed. "Can't wait to be out of here and back on the road."

Fela chuckled. "Not sure you can leave today. The press will want to interview you. Someone mentioned your name as the driver who brought the girls back. The story is you found them along the road."

"Good story," Law breathed. "Last thing I want is the press in my face. I've managed to avoid them so far. Once I can catch Temly's father alone, I should get the loan for our road trip back to Warri, and split."

"You may have to make a special arrangement. I'll tell Temly you need time with her father," Fela said. The girls were done, and the governor and his wife, along with Temly's parents, were next. "What time do you want to leave?"

"As soon as possible."

"What's the hurry? Asabi?"

"No. Your father. He was tied hand and foot, gagged, and blindfolded. How he escaped beats me."

"He has powers, Law. Keep it in mind. I guess it's a good reason to rush back to Warri. But not for me."

"I understand your concern."

Fela nodded toward the general room. "And Asabi? Will you tell me the story?"

"Someday."

"I know you will." He regarded his mentor. "She needs closure with her mother. Don't know what all this is about, but I thought you noticed, too."

"Yes, there's something there. And I'll find out, but I don't know when."

The priest made an announcement for everyone to come forward for the communion. Fela straightened. "Are you coming?"

"*Nah.*"

He searched Law's face. "God found me in the forest. I'm no longer one little brute encouraged to frustrate everyone while fighting his own gut."

Law arched his eyebrow for a split second and bowed his head. This meant a lot at the moment, knowing the foundation of faith was laid by the barber when he taught Fela's class in Sunday School. Now he was being preached at.

"I know how you feel—"

"You don't begin to scratch it, Fela." Law nodded toward the room. "Go and take the communion and say a prayer for me.

A word may have been appropriate, but Fela found none. He walked to the makeshift altar area and knelt beside others. After receiving his communion, he strolled back to where he'd been. Law was no longer there.

A tug at his heart sent him outside, and he found Law alone under a mango tree.

"I've been struggling not to take a smoke since we got here. Seeing her just brings back all the bad memories and cravings."

"Asabi's mom?"

"Yes. She looks so beautiful, like she hasn't aged one day."

"Don't tell me you still love her."

"I won't even argue."

"I think I can understand. I mean, I see Temly, and I'm alarmed at how emotional I get just looking at her."

Law chuckled. "Feeling like a man?"

"A married man." The two exchanged a knowing look. "I'm shedding this general guise. I'm done. I need to be a man."

The laugh drained from Law's face. "Happy for you."

"Are you going to talk to her?"

"I don't think so. Maybe you have noticed, but she's avoided me."

Fela shrugged. It was like old times again, when he and Law brainstormed issues as they came up in their lives. The age difference disappeared on the platform of concern.

"I don't know about these things, but under the circumstances, it is super awkward for you two not to at least say something to each other."

Law grunted. "It's been more than ten years. I'm sure I look every single day of those years, while she hasn't changed. And I'm sure she's wondering about my dreads."

Fela tried to make light. "I would, too. I can't imagine what Temly would do if she sees the picture in my room."

It worked. Law laughed. "You have to tear it down before she sees it, Fela."

"Before I see what?"

Temly stood about a foot away. She suppressed a smile. "You're talking about me. I know."

Fela chuckled. "Nothing you need to worry yourself about."

"He has this life-size portrait of himself—"

Fela grabbed his waist. "You can't talk."

"I can. I'm sure Asabi saw it, too."

"Law, you have secrets with me, too."

Temly laughed. "Someone would think you're two children."

Asabi walked up. "Everyone is looking for you, Temly. The service has ended."

Fela let go of Law. "Saved."

Temly rolled her eyes. "*Ahh*! I need a break. They keep asking the same question."

"Go on, dear. They need you inside," Fela shooed. "Come, let me escort you."

Temly shook her head but allowed him to take her hand. "I want to see the life-size portrait of you."

Chapter Forty-Nine

Asabi made a move toward the house.

"I plan to leave tonight. If I can have some time with Temly's dad." Law cleared his throat. "Just so you know. And be ready."

"I am ready."

"Also, I—well, I don't know how your mother's house is, but I wanted you to know I don't have accommodation in Warri."

Asabi sucked in her breath. "How is that possible?"

"I live in my shop. You've been there. It's nothing much."

"I don't care." She shrugged. "And you can get a place." She hesitated. "You've been giving so many excuses about this. If you don't want me, you can just say it."

"If I didn't want you, I wouldn't have told you who I am. You didn't recognize me."

She snapped. "Because you didn't want to be recognized. You posted a silhouette on your page, and you are nowhere else online."

"I did it to try and get your attention. And I did, so it worked—"

"You changed your name, too."

He grimaced. "No. My name is Lawrence Ola Ajayi. People got stuck with Law the barber—"

"And you didn't correct it. You didn't tell anyone your full name or put it on online."

"I don't want people finding me—"

She shouted. "Why? What are you hiding from?"

Since the service was over, the compound had filled up, and some people milling about glared at them. Breakfast was being served from several food booths, and there was a lot of chatter going on.

"Lower your voice, Asabi." Law sighed. "Let's find somewhere to talk."

He didn't wait for her and strode into the house. She contemplated for a moment and decided this was indeed a conversation she wanted to have. She entered the house but was accosted by her mother.

Eni exclaimed. "*Ah,* Asabi there you are. The priest wanted to offer special prayers for our family. Come along."

Asabi was not in the mood for pretense. Her head ached from everything. Who advised, or rather allowed, all these ceremonies around the house when what they all needed was psychological counseling and therapy?

She lashed out. "No. I will not come along." She licked her lips. "You can go along alone with your disgusting husband. I am not a member of your family."

Eni blinked. No one was in the dining area of the house where they were except for Law, who stopped his retreat and walked over to his daughter.

Eni gritted her teeth. "You don't talk to me like this, young woman."

She clenched her hands into fists. "*Oh,* of course I can. Did you notice my dad for a minute? Did you invite him to this special family prayer with the priest?"

"He is not a part of our family."

"You can't even look at him. You can't spare a glance to acknowledge him."

Law took her hand. "Asabi, there's so much between your mom and me. I don't blame her for being like this."

Asabi sneered. "See the kind, considerate man you left for, for—"

Femi Filips chose this ungodly moment to walk into the room. "*Ah-a,* Eni, the priest—"

"For this mean bastard!"

The three adults chorused. "Asabi!"

Law found his voice first. "Dear, come with me. You can't talk like this to a man who took care of you."

Asabi cried. "Don't defend them to me, Daddy. You don't know what I went through."

Eni raised her voice. "What did you go through, you ingrate? Femi took you like his own child and spoilt you. You go for vacation every year to the UK and America! You wear the best clothes, go to the best schools, live in a mansion—"

"I don't need your mansion and vacation." Asabi screamed. "You watch like you don't know what is going on. All you see is the money, you greedy—"

"Asabi!" Law clasped her hand. "Come with me."

She snatched her hand from his grip. From the corner of her eye, she saw Fela and Temly slowly walk in.

"No. How dare she tell me this nonsense? How dare she pretend I was taken care of by her and the brute she married?"

"People are hearing you, dear. We can talk about this—"

Temly's voice was low but strong. "Let her talk, Law. Please."

Tears gathered in Asabi's eyes. She couldn't. What did it matter anyway? Eni would deny it to high heaven, and she'd be the liar. Femi would take sides with his wife. They would shame her. Law's dark eyes squinted to slits, and though Temly may encourage her to speak out, she'd not live with the stigma.

"Yes, let her talk!" Eni shouted. "You are like your father, and I don't blame you."

"I am like my father, and I thank the *lord* I am." Asabi made to leave the room, but Law drew her back.

"Talk about what? What does Temly mean?"

She shook her head. "Nothing. It's okay. Excuse me."

Mr. and Mrs. Cole walked in. "The priest was looking for you," Mrs. Cole said to Eni. "Is everything okay?"

"Mom, Femi Filips rapes Asabi. He's been doing it since she was five."

Heat spread from her face through her entire body. "Temly, no." She tried to run as everyone except Femi Filips exclaimed, but Law tightened his grip on her wrist.

A low growl emanated deep from her father's belly. "He what?"

No one saw it coming. Law let go of Asabi's hand and jumped on Femi. The first punch caught the abuser on the jaw. Several others hit different parts of his face and landed him on his back. Law followed him down, despite efforts to pull him off.

Asabi wailed, and Temly pulled her into a hug and cried with her.

Eni shouted. "He will kill him. Don't let him kill him, please."

Asabi didn't know Law had such strength. Compared to Femi Filips, he was much slimmer, though a little taller. Mrs. Cole called in security men who succeeded and tore Law off the bleeding millionaire. He was handcuffed within seconds and taken out of the room.

Temly rushed after the men. "He didn't do anything wrong. Daddy! Stop them."

After what seemed like enough commotion to last a decade, Law was released, and Femi's beaten up body was taken to a clinic.

Everything went eerily calm afterward.

Chapter Fifty

"I didn't know I would be so outraged."

Asabi dipped a small towel in hot water and squeezed. She placed the hot cloth on Law's knuckles.

"I thought you would kill him."

"I would have." He cringed. "*Ah*, hurts."

"It has to. You bled, too."

"Are you sure we should use hot water. A cold compress is the right option."

"Either works."

He grunted. "How do you know?"

She chuckled. "I know. I attend a prestigious girls' school where they teach us everything."

He arched his eyebrow. "This is the first time I'll see you laugh."

She studied his hand and the angry swelling. "Not true."

He lifted her chin, forcing her to look at him. "True."

"Thank you for fighting for me."

He withdrew his swollen hand and sat back on the ladder-back chair propped against the wall in the guest room.

"I would die for you, Asabi. You're all I have." He swallowed. "I may not have given much when you were born, but my heart was always with you."

"No one has ever stood up for me. Ever." He searched her face, and though she had tears in her eyes, she giggled. "It felt good to see you beat him down."

"You are so beautiful, Asabi. I don't even know why anyone would hurt you in such a way."

She couldn't believe it, but he burst into tears. She moved closer and awkwardly put her hand on his back. The only time any man touched her with affection, it was wrong.

She didn't know what to do with her father. She wished she could jump on him have him pick her up like she'd seen Temly's father do so many times.

She heaved. "I'm sorry."

His head shot up. "Sorry about what? You never did anything wrong."

She shrugged. "My mother blames me."

He rubbed the back of his neck. "Why should she blame you? You were—are a child."

"She's never said it plainly but, well, she says stuff that add up to blaming me." She shook her head. "And sometimes he would come into my room when she was just across the hall in hers."

"You never screamed?"

"He threatened. Always did. He'd tell me how miserable my mother was when he met us. Sometimes he would put his head on my shoulder and cry. Beg me."

"Pervert."

"He always bought gifts for me afterward. He would thank me for loving him." Asabi sighed. "I stopped liking anything. Because once he got to know, he would buy it. I hated all colors. All food treats."

"How do you know your mom knows?"

"She knows. Even the housekeeper, Missis. She knows. But they keep quiet. They are afraid he will send them away. He's told me several times."

Law brought a shaky hand to his forehead. "Told you what?"

"If my mom complains, or any staff, he'd send them away. And keep only me."

"Did you ever try to tell your mom?"

She shook her head. "She—I never had the opportunity. I don't know when she first discovered, but she'd say things like what she was saying tonight, how he likes me a lot and I shouldn't spoil things for both of us by saying silly things from my warped imagination."

Law sat forward. "Did Eni talk about me?"

"Only to say you had no money and didn't care for me the way this man does. She never talked about you unless she wanted to compare you with her husband."

He heaved a heavy sigh. "I'm going to get a lawyer."

"No, Daddy. Please."

"I love it when you call me Daddy." He squeezed her hand. "And I am not going to let a pedophile go scot-free."

"He is rich. He'll fight you to the last."

"I know. But I won't go down easy. I won't let him think he can hurt my daughter in any way and escape without seeing a little bit of my wrath."

Asabi walked to the bed and sat on the edge. "I've watched movies with these issues, and in this country, the verdict will go to the highest bidder."

"I don't have any guarantees, but I won't give up before the battle begins." Law gingerly touched the ugly swelling on his hand. "I just hope I got some permanent damage in."

"You'll need me to testify in a court. And I'm not willing. Besides, I'd rather you use your money to get accommodation for both of us instead of paying a lawyer for a case you'll lose anyway."

"Thank you, slight taken."

"I like a man who knows when to give up."

He snickered. "I gave up once. I let Eni take you. Not again."

"Dad—"

He rose. "Something bothers me." He paced. "Did—did you ever get pregnant?"

Asabi gasped. The smile on her face disappeared. "I don't want to talk about it. And I won't cooperate with a lawsuit." She stood. "What time are we leaving tomorrow?"

He walked to her and knelt, his good hand gripped her foot. "Please, Asabi. I beg you."

"You won't believe it. No one does."

"Temly believes you."

"She's my friend!"

"I am your father."

She stepped away from him. "And you allowed my mother to take me away. You never cared to find me."

"I am sorry, Asabi! I was devastated when your mother left. For years, I had nothing except a tobacco addiction. And the moment I got my act together, I went online to search for her and did what I could to get to you." He rose and walked to stand before her. "Please, don't make me pay more than I already have." When she didn't say anything, he continued. "When was it? When did you get pregnant? Tell me. What happened?"

She took in a shuddering breath. "He uses protection all the time. Condoms. Last year, I don't know what went wrong. He said the product was—faulty." She closed her eyes. "Anyway, it tore. And I missed my period. I was about three months gone before I had the courage to tell anyone."

He drew her into his arms and patted her back. "Temly?"

"No. Only him." She sighed. "He gave me medication to take care of—of it."

Law whimpered like a trapped kitten. "Do you remember the name of the medication?"

"I took pictures of it." She bit her lip. "At the time, I thought I would show my mom but then I changed my mind."

"So, after you took the drugs, you lost the pregnancy?"

"Heavy bleeding. He rushed me to a private clinic, and zap. Finish. Done." She touched her forehead. "I need to rest. We have a trip tomorrow."

He nodded. "I'll see Temly's father. I hope he'll still agree to loan me some money."

Chapter Fifty-One

The following morning after breakfast, Law and Asabi got back on the road to Warri. It was a tearful departure. Fela wanted to stay behind with Temly, and in the aftermath of the day, her parents agreed.

He wasn't ready to face his father, but he advised Law to leave the Jeep where it could be recovered. "Let's keep quiet about everything until we find out what my dad plans to do."

Law nodded. "Okay, but I won't keep quiet long."

He bade Fela goodbye and drove out onto the highway.

Asabi tapped him. "Did you talk to my mom?"

"Yes."

"And?"

"Nothing." He shrugged. "She wanted to know how I found you, and I told her you found me. She didn't have many nice things to say."

Asabi rolled her eyes. "I want to know what she said."

"She hates my hair." He touched the dreadlocks. "Told me I was still a disgrace."

"What did she care?"

"What indeed." Law stole a glance at her. "Let's talk about our future, Asabi." He sighed. "I'm humbled you want to live with me. I will do everything to make you happy and comfortable. I may not have as much as your—"

Asabi kept her eyes on him, filled with joy she never imagined existed. "I don't care about what they have, you know."

Law inhaled. "I will get better living arrangements. And we'll get you into a nice school."

"You were reluctant to talk about it yesterday."

"Yesterday we were all emotional and sensitive. I wanted to have a plan to discuss with you today. And I wanted to be sure you hadn't changed your mind."

Asabi snickered. "I am here."

Law squeezed her knee. "And I am so glad, my dear."

They fell silent for a moment then Law cleared his throat. "Asabi?"

"Yes?"

"Should I cut my hair?"

She shrugged. "Well—I don't know. I guess you should."

Law laughed. "Okay, I will."

They chatted like they'd known each other during the whole trip. Before they both realized, they were on the outskirts of Warri.

"We're almost home. I'll call one of my customers who does real estate to find a good two-bedroom apartment for us."

"*Hmm*. Don't kill yourself over me. I will sleep on the floor if all you can afford is one room."

Law cackled. "No way!" They laughed.

He noticed a police checkpoint ahead and slowed down. An officer had the Jeep pull over and asked for Law's permits.

"Officer, this is not my vehicle. It's a long story, and I was taken from my shop without my wallet so my driver's license is not with me."

The officer snickered. "But you're driving."

"I had to."

"Who owns the vehicle?"

"Pastor Favor Peter."

The officer glared. "Excuse me." He walked to the police vehicle parked off the shoulder of the road.

Asabi and Law watched him talk to another policeman. Then he walked over to the Jeep with the other officer.

"You're under arrest. Pastor Peter has reported his Jeep missing."

"Can't be true. Pastor Peter knows the Jeep is with me. He is not—cannot—"

The policemen forced Law and Asabi out of the Jeep and cuffed them. They were both led to the police vehicle amidst Law's protests. One officer drove the police car while the other took the Jeep to the state police headquarters.

For the first time in Asabi's life, she slept in a police cell.

Chapter Fifty-Two

Fela leaned against the wall in Temly's bedroom but rocked back and forth, which made Temly dizzy as she sat up on her bed.

She leaned her head back on the headboard. "I'm sure they're fine, Fela," she said. He'd been restless all afternoon, and now he was beyond control. "Maybe he's busy."

"No, Temly. Law knows how important this is."

She cuddled her pillow. She just wished he would cool down a little. His nerves made her uncomfortable. A lot still needed to be done, and though her parents agreed he could stay in the guest room for as long as he wished, Temly knew he had to face his parents sometime.

"Law and I had a serious discussion last night. My father was tied up in the trunk of the Jeep all night, and he escaped before morning."

"Sounds so terrifying."

Fela knelt before her and gripped her knee. "Yes, it is. It unnerves me. Even more so because we haven't heard from Law. They should have arrived in Warri over four hours ago. Whatever could have kept them from calling can't be good."

"I hope Asabi is safe with him."

"Asabi is his long-lost daughter." Fela chuckled. "Even a stranger is safe with Law."

Temly felt relieved, though the truth around her friend's birth still puzzled her. Asabi had told her Law was a barber who owned a shop in Warri. She wasn't even sure he had a house of his own. Why she'd chosen to go with him amazed her. It only explained how much she hated her life with her mother. But she should have stayed back in Ibadan. Temly's home was always open, and she didn't think her friend had made a good decision to leave with a man she just met. What if he was abusive as well? Though the rage with which he tackled Femi Filips couldn't have been staged.

"Law is like my father," Fela said. "I can't just let anything happen to him right now."

He went to the living room where Mr. and Mrs. Cole lounged after a long day attending to guests who continued to pour in, including a delegate of staff and students from Temly and Asabi's school. Temly followed even though she still needed a lot of rest and couldn't walk well. Her parents divided looks between him and her.

In a shaky voice, Fela told them he had to leave. "Law came with my father's Jeep. It's a long story, but I need to go and find him. He should have called. It's unlike him not to call." The couple continued to stare at him, and he felt compelled to continue. "My father is not the typical kind of person. He is a wicked man." He swallowed. "He may harm Law and Asabi in an unimaginable way. I need to face him. Stop him."

Mrs. Cole spoke first. "We're sorry about your predicament. And worried about Asabi."

"If you need any money." Mr. Cole drew his eyebrows together. "We'll give you whatever you need, Fela."

"I do, thank you. I don't know how much I'll need, sir," Fela said. "But I have to get back. I have to find Law."

Temly touched his hand in reassurance. How this must feel for him after telling her parents about his father.

Mr. Cole shrugged. "I can give you ten thousand naira in cash right away."

Fela's face relaxed. "Thank you, sir. I'll make sure I repay every kobo."

"Won't be necessary," Mrs. Cole said.

Temly squeezed Fela's hand. "You need a cell phone, too."

"I'm sure I can buy one from the money your dad gives me."

Mrs. Cole shook her head. "I can give you my other cell phone. I hardly ever use it."

"Thank you so much for your help, ma'am." Fela patted Temly's hand. "Take care of yourself. I'll be back as soon as I can."

Mr. Cole exclaimed. "You plan to leave tonight? How?"

"Yes, sir. I wanted to see if I could start off tonight, and maybe—"

"Impossible. Even if you're driving your own car."

Temly stroked her chin. "Don't give me any farewell speeches. I'm coming with you."

Mrs. Cole gasped. "Of course not!"

"You don't think I'd let him go alone, Mom," Temly said. "After all he did for me. And Asabi is out there."

"You can't even walk properly." Fela shook his head. "I can take care of myself."

"I don't care what you say, Fela. Asabi told me what happened when they found you." Tears she couldn't control gathered in her eyes. "Mom, Fela could have been rescued. He refused to leave the forest till I was found."

"Don't be ridiculous. The situation was different."

Temly trembled. "I'm going to get my shoes and overnight bag." She walked to the door. "And if Fela leaves before I come back, I'll run away. And I mean it."

"Temly!" Mr. Cole's voice was hoarse. "Wait."

She stopped. He'd better say something good because she meant every word. She wasn't going to let Fela go alone to face his evil father. If he was right that Law and Asabi were in trouble, then she wasn't going to cuddle her teddy and sip hot chocolate while her friends faced unknown danger.

"Come here, child. Sit down and let's talk."

She refused to move. "No, Dad. This is what I want to do, and you can't change my mind."

There was an awkward pause while everyone exchanged nervous glances. To compromise or not. Temly watched her parents exchange glares, probably deciding whether to fight her resolve.

Fela scratched the base of his neck. "Temly. I have friends in Warri. I will go to them first. They will help—"

"No!" She continued with her limp toward her room.

She wondered how much help she'd be with a sprained ankle and the emotional trauma of all she'd experienced, but she couldn't stay in the comfort of home while some of her most important people faced danger. Real or imagined.

"We need to talk about the travel plans," Mr. Cole said. "I'm coming with you two."

"You're not!" Mrs. Cole banged her side stool. "Will you be reasonable?"

Temly couldn't conceal the wide smile on her face. Fela rushed to her and hugged her. She flushed and squeezed out of his embrace. Her father would not allow such behavior.

"I am reasonable," Mr. Cole said. "If I go with them, we'll have money, backup, and I will take one or two of our police guards with us."

Mrs. Cole sulked. "Do you know what you're dealing with? A cultist hiding behind the collar? The best we can do is ask your brother to take charge of the matter."

"Tai will be ready to send in one or two security details to assist, but nothing more. Our family is not his only concern in the state. And more is better than less in this case, darling. I am not about to lose any of these children." Mr. Cole stood. "Remember, Asabi is also in danger for all we know." He spoke to Fela and Temly. "I suggest we have dinner now and turn in early. We leave at dawn."

Chapter Fifty-Three

The Cole family and Fela travelled to Warri in two vehicles.

Fela found it both amusing and humbling. Mr. Cole took four policemen with him. The previous night, after the decision to go with Fela and Temly, Mr. Cole called his twin, the governor, who offered to put executive might behind their journey. Fela warned if this ended up being a state parade, his father would disappear.

What thrilled him most were the accommodations given them at the government liaison house in Warri. He'd never stepped in the complex before.

The team was welcomed by the district police officer (DPO) of the liaison house, and they checked into the guesthouse. Fela wished the circumstances were different. He anticipated a day when he could be a guest of the governor under normal circumstances.

Something had happened to Law and Asabi, and considering what his father could do, he shuddered at the thought.

After light refreshments, Mr. Cole called a meeting to strategize. "The governor told me he will give us all the help we need," he said. "So, Fela, what do you intend to do now?"

Fela cleared his throat. "I have to go home. See my parents."

"I understand." Mr. Cole nodded. "But is it safe? And in what way can we assist?"

"I have to go alone. I have to face them—" Fela choked on his words. Temly patted his hand.

Mr. Cole shook his head. "It's not all right."

"I can go with him."

Tayo, the last guy to respond because of his quiet nature, caught everyone's attention with his unexpected offer. Of Temly's two brothers, he was the younger and more timid. What use could Tayo be to him? If Fela needed an ally against his father, Tayo was the wrong one.

Mrs. Cole yelled, "No way."

Tayo shrugged. "Exactly. No one will believe we're together." He noted to the policemen. "If there's a way to wire Fela. I can be outside the house, loitering—"

"If this is your plan, Tayo, then a police officer can do it. Loiter," Mrs. Cole said.

"Monitoring Fela will not be a problem," the DPO said. "I'll arrange for two of my plain-clothes men to follow him."

Mrs. Cole's eyes shuttered closed for a moment. "Thank you, sir."

Fela echoed Mrs. Cole's sentiment with a smile.

The DPO clapped. "Now, you can relax. Fela and I will leave. We'll let you know how things go."

Mr. Cole nodded. "We trust you. Thank you."

Fela rubbed his nose. "Hey, Temly, where did you put my *kakaki*?"

Temly moaned. "Your *kakaki*?"

"Yes. I gave one to you in the bush. Did you leave it there?"

Mrs. Cole glowered. "What's *kakaki*?"

Temly's face lit in realization. "*Oh*. Sorry. Of course not. I didn't leave it." She gesticulated. "It's a small stem. We called it *kakaki* because we didn't know the name." She pulled Fela. "Come, I'll show you where I put it in your bag."

Fela hesitated. "No. You don't need to come with me. We don't have time. Just tell me which part of the bag."

"Unless I see it, I can't quite remember." She started to limp away before Fela could respond.

"It's my good luck charm. Please, let me just get it."

The DPO leered. "We don't have time."

Fela scuttled after Temly. "Just a moment, sir."

He entered his room ahead of her and pulled her into a big hug. "*Wow*, I thought you wouldn't get the message," he whispered. He closed the door and took Temly into the bathroom, closing that door, too.

Temly winked. "I'm a smart girl. What is it?"

"Temly, I'm scared." Fela licked his lips. "My dad is so—mean."

"I know. I'm sorry." She patted his cheek. "I'll be praying for you. And we're all here. You have your phone?"

He nodded.

"It will all end soon." Temly paused. "There's something I wanted to ask you. It's been bothering me."

"Ask."

"Asabi told me you're gay. And you wore makeup and prostituted for Law."

Fela cracked a laugh but held it back. "My parents told her, right?"

"She said your housekeeper told her."

"I'm not. I wore makeup to upset my parents. Law would never mess with anyone's mind. He's a decent guy. And he's been like a father to me."

Temly sighed. "Good. I told Asabi she was wrong. Now you got your *kakaki*, it's time to get into action. Where'd you get the name from anyway?"

Fela chuckled. "It's just a word. Popped into my head."

She hugged him. "Smart boy. Now let's rescue our precious Law and Asabi. I still plan to have a backup." She pulled back. "And the good DPO seems impatient."

"Temly." Fela's voice was sharper than he intended. "The *good* DPO is a deacon in my father's church."

Chapter Fifty-Four

The Peters were holding a special deliverance service when Fela, the DPO, and one plain-clothed officer found seats at the back of the church.

Papa Peter dressed in a bright red three-piece suit was in the middle of a prophetic spell. Many walked forward and fell at a touch of their foreheads by the man of God. His voice rang out through the auditorium like thunder. He denounced and blessed, cried and laughed. Yelled and spoke in soft tones.

Fela cringed at every word. How could one know a genuine man of God? There was so much display around his father, yet no one cared if he did his magic on the pulpit or not. People flocked to the church, and as long as they got what they came for, no questions were asked.

Was there no means of judging who should preach the word of God and lead people in the ways of righteousness? Fela knew he'd had an encounter with God in the forest, but short of starting his own church, where would he find the spirit and presence of God? He knew many of his father's friends in ministry were just as flamboyant, and he wondered what these men did in their closets. Did they have secret prayer rooms as well? Where was the fruit of the Spirit he'd heard of and read about in the Bible? Timeless truths he had learnt from the word of God were instilled in him by Law.

The service ended, and he followed the officers to his father's office, based on what the DPO suggested. Since Fela had allegations to make, it was better to make them in the presence of the officers here rather than at home. He'd hoped to have a private meeting with them, but it seemed he would not have the chance.

Papa Peter showed no emotion when the party of three entered his office. He narrowed his eyes, and his little smile sent shivers down Fela's spine. Had he known they would request to see him? The DPO went on his knees, as was the custom in the church when anyone sought audience with the preacher. The other officer followed suit.

Fela remained on his feet and glared at the man he'd called "Daddy" since he could talk, and he wished he had never known the man.

"Papa, I am blessed. Bless me, Papa." The DPO bowed to the ground. "Bless me, Papa."

Papa Peter's voice rumbled like the sound of many waves. "You are blessed."

Fela had often wondered how his father got this reverent tone. When he spoke at home, his voice didn't have such inflection.

"Bless me, too, Papa," the other officer said.

The officers' behavior stunned Fela. Were they under a spell?

"You have no right to bless anyone. You're wicked. You lied that you were going to a night prayer vigil and went into a forest to take part in a cult killing innocent people." Fela narrowed his eyes. "I have no respect for you, and until you confess, you cannot be forgiven."

The DPO rose to his feet in a flash and punched Fela in the belly. Fela reeled and slumped against the wall. Several heavy blows followed the first one until he slid to the floor, his arms shielding his body as much as he could.

"Leave him," Papa Peter said. "He thinks he knows a lot, but he knows nothing." He took a deep breath. "Bring me a keg of holy water. I will wash his head and free him of the demons."

Fela flared, his nose bleeding, lips split. "Your holy water means nothing. You will not escape this, Favor Peter. The devil you serve has lost the battle."

Papa Peter kicked Fela in the side and he gave a loud yelp. From the corner of his eye, he noticed the other officer was bowed down, and his hands covered his head in a protective manner. Fela wanted him to open his eyes and do his job but concluded these men must be loyal to his father. They must be bad men in police uniform.

"You fool."

The DPO came in with a full keg, and Papa Peter emptied the chilled water on Fela's head. He struggled to stand but couldn't.

Fela snapped at the DPO. "Why are you taking orders from him? You work for the police, not him."

The DPO snarled. "Shut up."

"You will leave us now and stand guard at the door. I don't want anyone to come in or out." Papa Peter changed his voice to the rumbling tone. "I have to exorcize my boy. It is painful but it needs to be done."

Mama Peter burst in, and Fela sighed. At least his mother would not watch his father hurt him.

"Deacon, leave us."

The DPO and the other officer left.

Tears came to Fela's eyes. "Mom, *oh* you're here." He clung to his mother's leg and battled tears.

"You useless child." Mama Peter shook him off. "You ungrateful element. After all we did for you! So, you sent one little animal, Asabi, to expose us?"

"Where is she?"

"You will never see her again." Mama Peter put her face close to Fela's. "We'd rather lose you and your friends than lose all—" She waved her hands in the air to signify the wealth around. "All—this. Do you hear me?"

"Mom, please. Help me. Help us. Don't allow him to change your heart. Don't allow Daddy to hurt us, please."

Papa Peter's voice came from a distance. "Tell him. I am not his father. Tell him now, Nkiruka."

Fela gasped. "What are you saying?"

Papa Peter jeered. "She doesn't know your father. She was a common prostitute when I married her."

"Whether you know or not doesn't matter anymore, Fela. I thought you would turn out with a little sense, but you are more like your real father," Mama Peter said. "Whoever he is."

Fela's stomach roiled with pain and anger and relief. "I'm glad he is not my father." He was now convinced she knew about her husband's associations and activities.

Fela closed his eyes. "What are you going to do with me?"

"Throw you away in the bin as I ought to have done when you were born." Mama Peter clenched her jaw. "Papa said you'd be no good, and he was right."

Fela opened his eyes. "Who's my father?"

"You'll never know," Papa Peter said. "Take him through the back to where his friends are. Let them all rot in Hell."

Fela sensed hope leave him. A back door? There was no back door he knew of. The auditorium had four entrances. Two at the front of the church and two side doors. His cell phone had been taken earlier by the DPO. He knew he was going to be in trouble but trusted Temly's backup plan would arrive on time to the rescue.

"God, I need Your help now. Do something, please—"

"Shut up," Mama Peter said. "*Oh*, so now you pray. Every day we pull you by the ears to come to the family devotion and you refuse. Now you pray?"

Papa Peter pressed his lips together. "Farewell."

Mom yanked him to his feet. Dare he struggle against his mother? This was a nightmare. A second nightmare.

He prayed, remembering how Asabi had encouraged them to pray in the forest and how he and Temly had cried to God when they were so sure death was near, and a strange peace came into his heart. If he died now, he knew Temly would continue to fight until his parents were arrested. It was a small consolation for him.

Mama Peter dragged him toward the wall behind Peter's desk and placed her left palm on a spot. Fela heard a soft click, and the wall opened. There was a noise outside the door to the office, and Mama paused.

Peter recoiled. "Bring him back—" But he didn't have a chance to finish his statement.

The DPO opened the door. "Papa, please forgive me. There are police vehicles everywhere. The church is surrounded. What are we to do?"

"Are you not a police officer? Protect us. Why do you think I made you a deacon?" Papa Peter snapped. "Do your job."

Fela didn't know where the strength came from. He pushed his mother so hard, she staggered and fell against her husband.

Before the DPO could attack him, he picked up a chair and threw it at the police officer. He missed. But he achieved his desire. The DPO took cover, clearing the entrance. Fela burst through the door and ran as fast as he could to the cover of true policemen.

Chapter Fifty-Five

One of the officers grabbed him. "What happened? Who are you?"

Fela couldn't respond fast enough. His words came out in stutters through a pounding heart. "He's there. In there. With Mom."

"Who?" The lead policeman didn't seem to understand why he and his team had been detailed to the church. "Identify yourself."

"You guys need to go in there before they escape."

"How many are there?"

He panted. "Four. Two are policemen."

The police officer gestured toward his colleagues. "The boy is not making any sense. Go and check this place out."

"The church, sir?"

The commanding officer snapped. "It's what this place looks like, isn't it?"

Ten men hurried into different sides of the church hall, guns drawn.

Fela blinked. "You may need more men, sir."

"Identify yourself!"

"My name is Fela. I—my mother is the wife of the pastor of this church." Besides the fact, he didn't want to identify himself as the son of such a tyrant. "He—the pastor is Favor Peter."

"*Oh*, this is his church? I've seen him on TV."

Fela slouched. Was this another Favor-Peter-crush? "This is his church, but he is not a true man of God. He uses powers, cultic powers, to destroy people."

The officer scrutinized the hall. Fela followed his gaze. There was nothing unusual about the building or the hall, except the fashionable and expensive display of colors. Nothing spooky, but Fela knew it was all a cover.   One of the policemen stepped forward. "The pastor was praying

"Is it what all this is about? Cultism? Do cult boys come here to hide?"

For the umpteenth time in one morning, fear gripped Fela's heart. This officer had no clue what he was faced with? Who sent him here? Was he Temly's backup?

"Sir, you need to understand something."

The officer walked toward the front of the hall toward the pulpit. He studied the seats and observed the floor. It didn't look like he heard a word of Fela's desperate explanation.

Two men walked briskly toward them. "Nothing, sir."

"All the members have left?"

"Yes, sir."

More policemen came out from the different angles with the same report.

Fela cried. "They are in the office. They couldn't have left, unless—there was a door. Mom touched the wall, and it shifted."

The commanding officer arched an eyebrow. "Come and show me."

He didn't want to go back into the office. His nose still bled, and his stomach cramped up, but he didn't see any way to get out of this.

He heaved a heavy sigh. "This way, sir."

A short corridor led to the office, with pictures of happy members and leaders hung on the wall. Fela noticed the commanding officer stop a couple of times to study them.

They got to the office, and Fela pointed. "This is it."

One of the policemen stepped forward. "The pastor was praying for two members when we came here. All is normal."

"All is not normal. They are not ordinary people!" Fela moaned. "He—they murder people and hide under God."

The commanding officer raised his hand to stop him and knocked. Favor Peter asked the visitor to come in.

The men entered. Fela cowered behind them. What was this operation all about? He couldn't remember the plan. Law and Asabi were still missing, and he had thought he would confront his parents about their activities and then go in search of his friends. Why was he here again?

"Police Detective Oghene. Pastor Favor Peter?"

"I am Favor Peter. This is my wife, Mama Peter." He pointed at her, where she sat beside him behind his desk. "Your men came to disrupt our service to God, and I would like to have an explanation. All morning, we have had to send members home, people who came to seek God."

"I have a warrant for your arrest, sir. You can explain when you get to our station."

This took Fela by surprise. Why was the Oghene man stalling all the while as though he didn't know what he was here for? He sighed and closed his eyes for a moment.

"*Ah*, at last. I'm sure it is in relation to my missing son? Did my wife tell you I am responsible for him being missing?"

Mama Peter stood. "He is responsible. My son has been missing for—"

Oghene motioned Fela forward. "Is this not your son?"

Mama Peter gasped. "What happened to you? *Ah*, my dear boy." She moved forward to hug him. She pressed his face into her chest, and he struggled to breath. "What did they do to you? Where did they find you?"

Fela stepped back and shouted. "He's escaping!"

It happened at the same time as Fela's alarm. Favor Peter pressed his hand against the wall behind him. The space shifted. In one swift movement, he stood and stepped in.

The wall closed in his face.

Chapter Fifty-Six

Temly paced the floor despite the pain she could feel in her ankle.

"Why don't you just sit down a bit? All will go well. Don't worry." Her mother pursed her lips. "There's nothing you can do except rattle all our nerves."

Temly rolled her eyes. She didn't expect any of them to understand. She felt guilty. Her family was here with her, safe in the welcome of the state governor, while Fela was out there, facing his evil parents alone, with policemen his father had allegiances with.

"I just wish we could do something more."

Mrs. Cole sniffed. "Like what?"

She shrugged. "I don't know. Tunji and Tayo could have followed in an unmarked car and sat across the street from the church just to see things." She'd tried to make such an arrangement with one of the policemen and promised to pay a charge later but would the man honor such a last minute unofficial request?

Mr. Cole laughed. "You were watching too many detective movies. Those are what Americans do, dear. Here, we just barge in."

Temly walked to the refrigerator at the corner of the sitting room and took out a bottle of water. She wasn't thirsty, but she needed to do something instead of exchanging words with her parents. They didn't understand.

Tunji came to her rescue. "I understand you, Temly, but right now, all we can do is wait and pray."

"They are taking forever. No one has given any feedback."

There was a knock on the door, and everyone focused on it.

Tunji raised his hands in the air. "Maybe there is the feedback we need."

The door opened before they responded, and two men in dark suits walked in. Close behind was their host, the governor of Delta state, with several more men in dark suits.

The Coles stood to welcome their host. He was a short, sturdy man in his middle age, and wore formal native attire, dressed much like Temly's uncle. She wondered if there was a dress code for state governors. His face was hard in a subtle way; she shuddered. His presence brought dread rather than comfort, and she wished she knew why.

"Good morning, Mr. Cole," the governor did not offer his hand. In fact, his hands were hidden inside his pant pockets. "I trust the family is fine."

Mr. Cole bowed. "Yes, sir. Thank you so much for hosting us at such a short notice." The rest of the family mumbled greetings.

The governor's eyes rested on Temly. She steered her gaze away. "Your daughter. She's the one who was missing?"

Her father stared at her. "Yes, sir. We are grateful she has been found. It was the most traumatic experience." He breathed. "But now her friend is missing and it's why—"

"I know."

The hard voice, the unnerving look, the hands in the pocket—she must be paranoid. She clasped her hands and summoned the scriptures of comfort and battle Fela taught her in the forest.

"This is why I came to see Temly," the governor said to Mr. Cole. "You all should go into the next room. I want to speak with her. Alone."

Her mother hesitated. They exchanged uncertain looks but finally gave in. Temly half-shrugged. Whatever the case, they would be behind the door.

One of the aides opened an adjoining door, and the family trooped in. Mrs. Cole gave Temly a small smile, which made her more anxious about the meeting. As soon as her family left, the aides went out the front door, leaving Temly alone with the governor.

"You were missing in the forest?"

The man took his hands out of his pockets, and though they seemed normal, a gold ring with a red stone caught Temly's attention. This was not an ordinary meeting. Her heartbeat increased. She imagined some awful things she'd watched in African movies about to happen, the African horror stints when man transformed into snake.

She bit her lower lip. "What do you want?"

The governor loomed over her. "*Ah*, you recognize power when you see it." He pointed to the front door where his men just walked through, and a man she thought she'd not seen before entered, dressed in a long robe.

For a moment, however, her memory served her. This was the man the pregnant woman acknowledged before she was taken to her ill fate.

"Favor Peter."

The name hung off her mouth for a moment.

Fela's father.

Chapter Fifty-Seven

The world around Fella began to spin and he fought to hold onto consciousness. As he struggled unsuccessfully to break free of his mother's embrace, his eyes rolled to the back of his head, and his throat dried up. Would she actually kill him in front of all these witnesses?

She screeched. "Don't let him escape. He tried to kill my son."

Men's footsteps scuttled around the large office and Detective Oghene exclaimed, "There's no door. He entered the wall."

Doors slammed and Fela knew the men had run for their lives. The Nigerian police may be known for a lot of things but capturing voodoo-disappearing criminals wasn't one of them. Anyone who saw it would run for dear life.

Mama Peter continued to squeeze the life out of him, but he didn't know what to do. None of the officers seemed to notice he'd gone limp in her embrace. Would she let them leave with tales of what they had seen?

Certain the few remaining minutes of his life were hanging by a thread, he summoned the Word of God to his rescue. *Even though I walk through the valley of the shadow of death, I fear no evil; for thou art with me; thy rod and thy staff, they comfort me.*

I am not afraid of ten thousands of people who have set themselves against me round about—

When you pass through the waters I will be with you; and through the rivers, they shall not overwhelm you; when you walk through fire you shall not be burned, and the flame shall not consume you—

Where the words came from, he didn't know, and somehow, he was still alive. A sudden calm overcame him. All the men must have left. Still, his head remained clamped in his mother's strong grip, and tears streamed from his eyes. He could hold his breath no longer, and his tight chest failed him.

His mother must have comprehended his plight or assumed he was out. She freed him, and he slumped to the ground. Laughter thundered through the room.

He lay in a heap waiting for her to leave so he could drag himself to freedom. If it were possible. God had again spared his life.

She kicked him in the side. "Stand. I know you're still alive."

He'd thought the confrontation would be with both parents but as it was, that likely would never happen. It didn't matter anyway. All he wanted now was to escape from this nightmare and pick the pieces of his life again. Find a place in another town, work, and serve God. He didn't imagine he could continue with his education till his life had a direction.

He raised his head. "Why?"

"Why?" She laughed. "Why else? Power, of course. Power."

"You had everything. What do you need power for?"

"You are stupid, and you ask too many questions," she said as she sat down behind the desk her husband had just occupied. "If you were not so inquisitive and stubborn, you would have inherited this. Your life would be on top. Nothing would be able to control you."

"Your husband controls you, so what is the essence of your power?"

Fela squeezed the small ring in his palm. It had come off his mother's clothing as he gripped her, struggling for his life. He traced it with his fingers but there was nothing special. It was small and smooth.

She laughed. "The opposite. I tell him what, where, and when. All the power would have been yours, but you messed it up." She stood and felt her body as though searching for something. For a moment, she fretted and heaved a heavy sigh. "Well, I am going to leave you here and go find those cowardly policemen. And don't bother moving — your life is tied to me. When I blow out your candle, you will join your friends in eternity."

Fela swallowed. "Where are they?"

She walked to the spot where she'd been holding him and searched the floor.

"Where did you put my friends?"

"I will leave now," she said. "My sister would have taken your sisters to our safe house. Even your father doesn't know the place."

"You said he's not my father."

Fela rubbed the ring in his hand. Was she looking for it? What was it to her? He pushed himself off the floor and leaned against the wall. His mother walked to the magical space behind the desk and pressed her hand against it. It didn't shift back as it had done for her husband.

Frantic now, she searched her clothing and swirled around.

He held up the ring. "Are you looking for this?"

She surged toward him. "Fela. Give it back." She held out her hand. "Give it to me before you hurt yourself."

She stepped closer, and he punched her face.

Chapter Fifty-Eight

"You defied death once, but you can't do it again. I thought I'd have to travel the world to find you, but you made it easy coming to me."

Temly sneered at him. She thought she'd be afraid. Instead, she felt an assurance. She had indeed come into the lion's den, and God would shut their mouths for her sake. Things did not just happen. God had a plan.

She ignored Favor Peter's words and focused on the governor instead. "I will make sure my uncle knows the kind of person you are."

Both men laughed. "Your uncle, indeed," Favor Peter mocked. "Who is your uncle? When you and your family will be dead, and the good governor here will dispose of you all without a trace."

Temly didn't flinch. "Speak, governor. We came here for your help."

The governor ignored her and stood in front of Favor Peter. "I have delivered them into your hands as you demanded. Let me go, please."

"You have done well," the evil pastor said. "Now bring them out, kill them one by one, and you are free."

"You think I will stand here, and have you order my family's execution?" Temly didn't know where her strength or boldness came from. She recoiled for a minute. Something wasn't right.

"Use your power and kill them. There won't be blood. I am still a political leader. I don't want any of this to lead to me."

The blubbering rankled, but Temly seemed to be the only one in control of her wits. She watched the two men.

"Rub your ring. You will disappear. No one will remember you came here."

"You rub your ring."

Temly couldn't stay quiet when it seemed something she didn't quite understand was going on. She raised her voice and began to recite Psalm Twenty-Three, the only scripture she could think of. The door to the adjoining room opened, and her father stepped in.

"Daddy, pray. Pray," she yelled. "Even though I walk through the valley—" The rest of the family walked in and joined her to recite the Psalm.

The two men continued to argue.

The governor stated, "I didn't have anything to do with this. If only you had left things as they were and hadn't gone about making so much noise."

Peter yelled. "You wanted to be governor at all cost, and I gave you what was needed. Now you don't want to sustain it. This is your fault and yours alone."

Unexpectedly, everything began moving. Mrs. Cole's hand flew to her chest. "They have lost their minds, speaking their secrets with us here."

Tayo began a video recording as the two powerful men spoke about their wicked activities, trading blame.

Mr. Cole called one of the men from his brother's squad. "You need to come and arrest the governor and another man."

It must have been the call or the speed the security men came in with. The governor's men followed and tried to prevent their boss being handcuffed while he continued to blubber. Temly thought Favor Peter would use the opportunity to escape, but he stood there and spoke of how he hated it when men couldn't stand by their own decisions. Some reverse spell seemed to work on the two evil men.

A scuffle ensued between Mr. Cole's man and the governor's man. One of them pulled out his service weapon and fired.

The last thing Temly heard was a piercing scream.

Chapter Fifty-Nine

Fela couldn't move his feet if it would save his life. He slid to the floor beside his mother's fallen figure and wept.

His punch had been defensive and weak, but she had dropped flat on her back. It couldn't have killed her, and she wouldn't be knocked out for long. He needed to find his friends, or at least get out of there. Temly would be worried.

First, he had to open the wall. Whatever was behind it needed to be exposed. Favor Peter had gone in and remained there. Fela clutched the magic ring in his hand and crawled behind the desk. With ring in hand, he pressed the wall. Nothing happened. He drew himself up on his feet and pressed a wider area, and to his astonishment, the concrete shifted.

He moved back, and the wall shut. He didn't want to enter and find he couldn't return. Unsure if it would help, he dragged over his father's swivel chair, opened the wall, and used the chair to wedge the space open. It worked.

He murmured words of prayer, stole his mother a glance as she was still out, and stepped across the threshold.

A small passage led through an opening without a door, into a large dank hall. It was dark so he waited for a minute to accustom his eyes. What he saw heaved up everything in his stomach, and he spent the next several moments puking.

When he thought he could straighten, he returned his gaze to the seemingly endless space filled with human remains. There were bodies in different stages of decay. Fela coughed and spat as his gaze roamed the expanse as far as he could see. He didn't think he could walk through, so he changed direction to see if there was another exit besides the one he came through. There had to be. Favor Peter was nowhere in sight, and though he could disappear and reappear at will, Fela believed there had to be another way out of this place.

He needed illumination. He rushed back to the office and found his mother's cell phone on the desk. He switched on the flashlight and returned to the hall of death.

He gasped. The room wasn't as big as he'd thought. Just about twice the size of a standard living room. There wasn't any furniture, but bodies were flung all over the floor. Skulls and skeletons in the mix told him his parents had been in this business for a long time. Along the four walls of the room he noticed stakes and something else.

Two of the stakes had people tied to them. He picked his way closer and exclaimed.

"Law!"

He tripped over something slimy and fell face down. The stench about took him through another bout of nausea. He pushed up, swallowing hard, and walked with more alertness toward the first stake.

He sobbed. "Law." He touched the base of his neck and found pulse. "Law."

He stuck his light under his chin and loosened the rope around his mentor. He glanced over and noticed Asabi was tied several poles away.

Law murmured. "Is she alive?"

"I will have to check."

Law fell on him and would have brought them both down had Fela not mustered all his energy.

"Please check," Law whispered.

"You have to try and stand. I can't carry you."

Law groaned. "My legs don't work. I think they're broken."

Fela sniffed. "This is a death house. I—let me tie you back and check Asabi."

He wound the rope back, his mind reeling. How was he going to get them across this dingy room? He managed to get to her and cupped her chin.

"Asabi? Can you hear me?" She didn't respond. He patted her cheeks. Her head lolled. He felt for a pulse but couldn't find one. "Don't die, please. Not now."

He used his teeth to hold the phone so he could have better use of his head and hands and loosened the rope around her.

He heaved her on his shoulder. "*Ugh grr.*" He dropped to his knee, and only by sheer will pushed up. She weighed a ton. He staggered toward Law.

He couldn't speak now. Law raised his head. "Is she alive?"

Fela nodded and swung his head toward the way he'd come. If he could take her to the office, he would return for Law.

He stopped short at the reflection of light. Someone else was inside the room now, too.

Chapter Sixty

Fela froze when the light hit his face. It was a strong one, and he closed his eyes on reflex. Now death had come to him. He couldn't escape this time. At least he'd tried his best. Favor Peter had closed in.

"Fela! What are you doing here?"

The voice was not familiar but congenial enough it didn't matter. "Please, help us."

The bearer of the light moved closer. He discovered there were two of them.

"Take the girl from him," the voice said in a commanding tone.

The weight came off, and he near slumped. He didn't need to ask for help with Law. The rescuer untied him and heaved him up. Fela reckoned he must be a big man to carry Law with just a hurl.

"Come, quick," the man said.

He found there was a third person. The man who carried Law wasn't the leader of the group. *They must be policemen*, Fela thought.

They returned through the wedged wall into the office where Mama Peter sat propped against the wall, her eyes so bright she might be high on some cheap drug.

She chanted, "Close the place."

Law and Asabi were taken away to receive urgent medical care. Fela kept an eye on the man who'd assisted him to get out. He was sturdy and a little older than his father. He wore a collar, too, and a slight potbelly bulged under his black shirt and trousers.

A pastor?

Fela leaned against the wall. "Who are you, sir?"

The man wore a sad smile. "I am the president of an association of Christian leaders in this city. Your father called me Bishop. My name is Goodness Orji." He sighed. "I didn't expect you to know me because your father has told me how you refused to be converted."

Fela closed his eyes. Whatever. "Thank you for helping us. How did you know? All the policemen ran away."

"I believe someone called my number to tell me police were raiding the church. It is my duty to intervene."

"What a blessing."

"You need medical help, too." He moved toward the entrance beside the ranting woman. "Let me call my driver."

"No, don't go, sir."

The seething continued. "Close the wall. Close it."

"I'll be back—"

"No, sir. Sit. Please. Do you know what is going on? My mom, this open wall, this church? Favor Peter went through and disappeared."

"Son, let's just be glad this mess is over. Right now, you need to get to the hospital."

Fela closed his eyes. He needed rest. With the adrenaline no longer pumping through his veins, all the pain seemed to settle in. Splitting didn't begin to describe his headache, and Bishop was right, things may be damaged in his body.

"What about her?"

Bishop's voice was so soft Fela opened his eyes to better hear him.

"I think all the evil they've done has made them go crazy. I've seen it happen before. She loses her mind when the spell is broken by force." Bishop shook his head. "It is a tragedy. I knew they were not doing something right, but this? This beats me into total shock."

"And in there? All those dead bodies?"

"You would have joined the number."

Fela sniffled. "I must have torn the ring off her skirt when she strangled me. I think it's the power behind everything she does."

Bishop muttered. "Where's the ring?"

Fela pointed at the swivel chair holding the wall back. "I reckoned whoever had the ring could open the wall, so I kept it on the wheel of the chair. I think it worked."

A group of policemen marched in.

The lead greeted them. "Good afternoon, Bishop. Thanks for calling."

"Thanks for coming, officer." Bishop pointed toward the opening. "Keep the chair wedged if you don't want to be locked in."

"We will be careful."

Fela flinched. "You need a lot of light to count the bodies, too."

"Can you tell us what is going on?"

Bishop straightened. "It's a long story, but a ring keeps the wall open, and we don't know if there's another exit."

Fela walked to the chair, took out the small ring from where he hid it, and pulled the chair away. The wall closed. The policemen jumped back. Just as he did earlier, he hit the wall, and when it opened, he wedged it, put the ring on the seat, and ambled to Bishop.

The new lead officer smirked. "My demolition team will come and break down the walls. We don't know about rings, Bishop." He marched out the way he came.

Fela sighed. "Sir, please take me to the hospital."

He fainted before he heard Bishop's response.

Chapter Sixty-One

Fela sucked in his breath when he entered Asabi's private hospital room with Bishop and Mrs. Orji.

Asabi lay near death. Her face was bruised and bandaged, her arm in a cast. Would Temly's friend survive? Now he understood why Bishop had tried to prevent him from visiting earlier.

He stood rooted at the doorway. "Will she live?"

Bishop nodded. "She will, son. Her injuries are not as bad as she looks. The doctor says she'll be able to sit in two weeks."

He gasped. "Two weeks!"

What kind of person would do this to a teenage girl? How more or less serious were Law's injuries if Asabi survived with this much damage?

"She is lucky, Fela. You reached them when you needed to." Mrs. Orji rubbed his back. "An hour or two later, and they would not have made it."

Bishop clasped his hands. "Your father did worse than anyone imagined. And he hid it well."

Fela lowered himself into a chair. "Dad always had *friends* in the police and military. He surrounded himself with protectors."

"A dungeon in the *church* premises. It was a cover-up of the underworld. Again, the Body of Christ has suffered a blow," Bishop said.

Fela blinked back tears. "When I saw the DPO, I knew I was doomed if I didn't get help."

"I don't expect less from a church member like the DPO." Mrs. Orji clapped. "Faithfuls, they are called. He believed your father was not involved in the cult."

Fela moved close to the bed. "Asabi. Poor dear. She's been through so much. And all for Temly."

Bishop patted his back. "She'll be fine. We came just in time. Can you imagine what would have happened?"

"I would never have been able to drag them out." Fela shrugged. "God worked everything out for good." He sucked in a quick breath. "All this tragedy just because of men's greed and wickedness." He swallowed. "Can we go and see Law now?"

Bishop nodded. "Yes."

Mrs. Orji searched her husband's face. "How is he though?"

"A little better than Asabi. He was beaten near to death, too, but he's strong now."

Temly walked into the room with Tunji and burst into tears. Fela leaped to his feet and was at her side within a second, gripping her in a side hug.

"She'll be fine, Temly. I called your number from the hospital—"

"He didn't make it, Fela." She wailed. "*Oh,* my goodness."

Fela frowned. "Who? Law?"

Tunji swallowed. "My dad. He was shot yesterday." Amidst the struggle to hold his tears, he explained what happened. "We were told Asabi was here. Temly wanted to see her before we head back home."

Fela fought tears. "Why, *oh* no! He came here because of us. How could this happen?"

Temly sniffed. "Will Asabi be okay? I can't take any of this anymore, Fela." She wailed into his chest.

Bishop stepped forward. "I'm sorry for your loss."

Tunji nodded. "We have to go. Uncle sent the state house ambulance this morning. We leave immediately."

"How's your mom?" Fela stuttered. "She never wanted us to embark on this journey."

"She's stable now." Tunji pulled Temly away from him. "We need to go."

"I will come to Ibadan as soon as I can. Today or tomorrow."

Tunji shook his head. "No. I think you'd be better off here. To clean up your mess." He marched out of the room with his sister.

Tunji's words shook Fela to his core. Short of being blamed for their family tragedy, he knew he had just been told he was no longer welcome in their home.

Chapter Sixty-Two

Fela stepped out of Bishop's Jeep; his knees wobbled. It seemed like forever since he called this place home. Two police vans blocked the gate with armed men on duty.

Bishop walked up to the men and identified himself. After a brief interaction, the officers allowed him to enter the compound with Fela. One of them escorted the duo into the main house.

They stepped into the lobby, and Fela noted how changed the house was. To think it was only yesterday everything exploded on their serene and affluent existence—well, his parents'. His journey had started much earlier in the month.

Nothing was the same. The home had been searched and was not as tidy as Fela knew it to be. The furniture in the sitting room was torn apart. His mother would have had a fit to see her beautiful and expensive leather seats slashed like garbage.

He led Bishop and the policeman down the long corridor, past his parents' bedroom to his. He had only one thing in mind—to tear down the life-size portrait, which no longer represented who he was.

His door was open, as were all the other doors he passed by, evidence the police or whatever authority had entered here, too. To his relief, the portrait had been taken down and left on the floor, half-torn.

He picked it up. "This is the only reason I came here." He swallowed. "To destroy this." He spread it out and watched the eyes of his companions widen.

"Your father said you were wayward, but I never imagined—"

"He's not my father, sir. But it is a story for another day."

Bishop lifted his chin. "What happened to you?"

Fela heaved a heavy sigh. "After he—Favor Peter—tried to break my head when I was thirteen, I decided I would do everything to embarrass him. His image was so important to him."

"You did a good job, boy." Bishop sighed. "How old were you here?"

"Fifteen. This was last year. I told Law I needed a makeover. He practiced the art of make-up on my face." Fela chuckled. "The lady in the hairdresser's next to his shop loaned us the cosmetics and taught us how to use it."

"*Hmm*. You look perverted from top to bottom. Any father would have been devastated to see his son like this."

Fela arched an eyebrow. "Do you have a son, sir?"

"Two. So, I know what this could have been like."

"Except you love your sons. This man hated my guts from the start. And I reciprocated."

"I'm glad you have come out of this stronger."

"Yes, sir." He dragged in a shuddering breath and found a pair of scissors. "Well, goodbye world." He shredded the poster. "Thanks for coming here with me. I think I have the closure I need."

On the way out, he stopped at the entrance to his parents' room and peeked in. The room was a total mess. He imagined the investigators would have spent a lot of time there looking for anything to incriminate them.

"Do you know if they got a confession? I mean, the police?"

Bishop shrugged. "The officers gave statements, but I understand your parents have been quiet. The evidence is overwhelming. I believe they will both be charged in court for multiple counts of murder."

"Law told me the detectives who questioned him said there was no code for voodoo. You can't charge a man for blowing smoke into your eyes and disappearing on you."

"It seems. But with the number of skeletons in the church, there's no escaping the hangman. Sorry to say."

Fela pressed his lips together and stepped back. "There's one more room. Where it all started." He opened the door next to his parents'. It was empty. He didn't want to step inside, afraid the spell could still work. "Goodbye."

He blinked so he would not cry and led the men back to the gate.

"They will, without a doubt, pull this down." He squinted. "I will never come here again."

"My offer remains open, Fela. You can come and live with me and my family. At least till Law gets better and for as long as you wish."

"Law has his daughter now, and they'll live together. I know he will want me to stay with him, too. But I doubt he can afford it."

"This is why my home will remain open to you. And to him."

Fela stuttered. "You don't know what this means to me. To have nowhere to go, and yet you throw your doors open to me."

Like a child who had missed the most important moments in his life, he felt vulnerable. He took a small step toward the man of God who pulled him into a hug.

"You are a great child, Fela. And God will have a field day using you for His glory."

Epilogue

Temly took the microphone from her uncle, the executive governor of Oyo State, and mouthed *thank you* as her two-thousand-strong audience roared with applause.

The blue dress her mother bought her for this occasion was slim-fitted and comfortable. It made her feel grown up. Today, she and her friends launched "Kenny's Child," in memory of her late father, a new organization to help keep children in distress safe with their families.

Asabi sat on a high stool with a sad smile. The ugly scars on her face little diminished her beauty but served as a reminder of what a survivor she was. She wore an identical dress to Temly, though hers was white. She had chosen the color because she felt her life was brand new. Though she'd been discharged three weeks after her initial stay in the hospital, she still walked with a cane.

Law sat beside Asabi in a wheelchair. When he'd said he doubted his legs could work a year earlier, Fela had thought it was out of pain and weakness. In fact, he had been so injured it affected his spine. Doctors had told him he might never walk again.

Fela, on the other side of Law, wore a dark suit and sparkling white shirt; his hair was shaved to the scalp. Temly thought he was too handsome with his new look.

"Exactly a year ago, my father was caught in a crossfire. He was killed," Temly said.

She made eye contact with some of her listeners, of which many were university students and human rights activists. She was grateful her uncle facilitated the event.

"I have been told I may never recover from the experience, and I pray I never will. Because the singular event marked the end of an era in my life and the beginning of a new one." There was spattered applause. "I met great new people—" She beamed at Law and Fela. "And old relationships were strengthened." She beamed at Asabi, who returned the gesture.

"Today, I am not just a mommy's girl anymore." She caught her mother's gaze where she sat flanked by Tunji and Tayo on the front row of the hall. "I am a young woman in battle." The crowd applauded. "After going through what I did, I am now at war against every form of child neglect and abuse. I am a warrior fighting an ongoing war!"

Emotions clogged Temly's throat as the audience screamed and clapped. She never expected this much support. Looking through the crowd, she tried to gather her composure. She saw the principal of her school and a whole section of her fellow students, all clad in their uniforms. It had been tough to go back to school when she had lost almost a full term recovering from her trauma. Her principal had been gracious to let her return when she could and sit for the exams she missed. Their support moved her to continue. She was doing the right thing at the right time in the right place.

"No child deserves to be abused at home or anywhere else. We are launching a war against every form of child abuse." She valued the people on the high stools, who'd stood by her through all of this. Her uncle and his wife, governor and first lady of the state, Fela, Asabi, Bishop Orji and his wife, who continued to provide the spiritual nourishment they needed, and the chairman of Kenny's Child, Law.

"My hope is renewed. I see a new Nigeria where children go to school, not roaming the streets with trays of goods on their heads in the rain or in the heat of the sun." Temly moistened her lips. "Those children are the ones most vulnerable to ritual killings, kidnapping, and sexual abuse. Our war is against adults and parents or anyone who does not care!" Thoughts about Asabi's mother made her pause. The woman had since married another man, and no one had heard from her in a while. "Mothers--who trade the peace and wellbeing of their children for a good life--a *so-called* good life.

"Today, my friends celebrate with me. We do not see our work as trivial, though it is a small beginning. With the help of our sponsors and patrons, Kenny's Child succeeded in getting a conviction and jail term for the pedophile millionaire, Femi Filips. And deceptive church leaders who hid behind the collar to kill people for money and power are today both convicted and awaiting execution."

Temly beckoned Fela and Asabi, and they walked over to flank her at the podium. She held them both at the waist. "Today, we officially launch Kenny's Child as we remember a true and loving father who paid the ultimate sacrifice for the peace and stability of his child. We say an end is here for child abuse and forced labor. We begin a new fight against kidnapping and ritual killings. We seek your support from home and abroad—" Temly fought to keep the tears from flowing, but she couldn't.

Fela took a white handkerchief from his pocket and gave it to her, and she received it with a slight nod of appreciation. Sweet Fela. She was madly in love with him. And she believed he loved her, too, but they were still too young. Who knew what lay ahead? For now, it was enough being his best friend.

They would live in different cities, she in Ibadan and Fela in Warri with Law and Asabi. She had thought it was safer for them to move to another city, but Law wanted to stay in Warri and fight whatever came their way, and Fela and Asabi stayed where he did. She comforted herself knowing she would go to university wherever Fela chose.

"We want this fight to be everyone's fight," Fela said while Temly sniffed and wiped the tears from her cheeks. "We now have offices in Warri and Ibadan, and we will open others in Lagos and Abuja soon. Fliers with our office addresses and contacts are being distributed right now."

Temly watched uniformed ushers move across the rows. She thought Fela's voice was deeper now, but she might just be magnifying one of the things she loved about him.

"Call at any time of the day or night to report suspected forms of abuse against children you know. If you are the victim, please feel free to contact us," Asabi's voice rang out strong and determined. Temly was so proud of her. "We are fighters. Together we will win."

Asabi took Temly's hand and raised their clenched fists in the air. Temly did the same with Fela. The audience rose and imitated their gesture.

"Thank you," Temly said.

She hugged Fela and Asabi tight, sobbing at the success of their launch and the magnitude of the fight ahead.

Nigeria was such a large country, with over one-hundred-and-sixty-million citizens, of which at least forty percent were children. But an end to this hawking and abuse had to start somewhere.

Temly raised her head and murmured to her friends. "We may not be able to do it all on our own. But together we can make a difference!"

The End.

Thank you for purchasing my book. If you enjoyed this novel, *Under A Red Delta Sun*, please leave a review here: https://www.amazon.com/review/create-review/?asin=B085ZV48HS

Thanks again!

Also by Sinmiṣọla Ogúnyinka

- Blue Dawn

- Frail Flesh

- Scent of Water

- Her Lover

- Pepper

- Foreverland

- The Days after that Night

- Tisha

- I'll Tell My Story

- Way of the Unfaithful

www.ingramcontent.com/pod-product-compliance
Lightning Source LLC
Chambersburg PA
CBHW030937210726
48290CB00007B/2219